CHARTER MARK

Awarded for excellence
to Arts & Libraries

Kent
County
Council

DRIVEN BY LOVE

Four years ago, Andrea's fiancé, the handsome Austrian racing driver Josef Meyer, had broken her heart. She had vowed then that she would stay well away from him in future, but now he was back in England to race for her father. Josef told Andrea that he had heard her father's business was in trouble, and he suggested that he should help her find out what was going on. As her father looked so ill, this was an offer that Andrea knew she couldn't refuse.

Books by Suzanne Clarke
in the Linford Romance Library:

CHANGE OF HEART
SECOND CHANCE
ONCE IN A LIFETIME
STORMY PASSAGE
IN SEARCH OF LOVE

SUZANNE CLARKE

◆

DRIVEN BY LOVE

Complete and Unabridged

LINFORD
Leicester

First published in Great Britain in 1997

First Linford Edition
published 2004

British Library CIP Data

Clarke, Suzanne
    Driven by love.—Large print ed.—
    Linford romance library
    1. Love stories
    2. Large type books
    I. Title
    823.9′2 [F]

    ISBN 1–84395–266–1

Published by
F. A. Thorpe (Publishing)
Anstey, Leicestershire

Set by Words & Graphics Ltd.
Anstey, Leicestershire
Printed and bound in Great Britain by
T. J. International Ltd., Padstow, Cornwall

This book is printed on acid-free paper

1

Andrea was surprised to hear a knock on her bedroom door as she was towel-drying her long, blonde hair. Pulling her satin wrap around her, she went to answer it.

'What is it?'

'You've got a visitor,' Dave, one of her two flatmates, whispered.

She sighed with annoyance.

'Dave, could you ask them to go away, please? I've got to get to my dad's office for a nine o'clock meeting. I could call them later today.'

'He was very insistent, Andy. I don't think he'll go until you see him.'

Mick, Andrea's and Dave's other flatmate, grinned sheepishly and bid them good-morning as he headed to the bathroom. Andrea's attention returned to Dave and she wondered why he looked slightly astonished.

Shrugging her shoulders, she tied the satin belt firmly at her waist and padded downstairs.

As soon as she entered the lounge, her body tensed on seeing the back of the man who was looking at their garden through the patio windows. In a split second, all the hurt she'd felt four years ago came flooding back.

Sensing her arrival, the tall man with thick, dark hair turned around slowly.

'Hello, Andrea.' His voice was as velvety-smooth as she'd remembered.

'What are you doing here, Josef?' she uttered in disbelief, watching him as he strolled towards her.

'I thought it best if we talked before this morning's meeting,' he replied, his Austrian accent still discernible. As his gaze travelled leisurely over her dishevelled appearance, a smile played on his sensual lips.

'What do you want?' she snapped, tugging at her wrap and wishing she'd changed before coming down.

'Is that any way to greet an old

friend, Andrea?' he countered, raising his eyebrows mockingly and sitting in one of the armchairs.

It was hard for her to believe this was the man she'd fallen so deeply in love with five years ago.

'I need a cup of coffee. Can I get you one?'

'Please. Black with one sugar.'

As if she'd forget! In the kitchen, she waited until the kettle boiled rather than return and make small-talk with the man who'd turned her life on its head.

'Is that who I think it is, Andy?' Dave said, joining her in the kitchen.

'Probably,' she muttered, grimacing.

'You never told me you knew Josef Meyer!'

'He began his racing career with my father's company,' she told him, pouring hot water into the mugs. 'I'll tell you all about it another time, Dave.'

She hadn't advertised the fact to her house-mates that her father, along with her uncle, owned the majority of shares in one of the smaller Formula One racing teams. Since breaking up with Josef, she had purposely distanced herself from the sport as the hurt and humiliation she felt then was still just as strong. And now Josef was back — but why?

Taking the mugs to the lounge, she set Josef's down on the table.

'You haven't changed much, Andrea,' Josef remarked once she'd sat down.

'You have.'

She recalled their first meeting at her father's factory when Josef had been dressed in faded jeans and a battered, leather, bomber jacket. Immediately she had been struck by the raw sensuality of the tousle-haired, twenty-five year-old Austrian as he'd smiled at her. Five years on, Josef was just as handsome, though now he was a very different person sitting there in his designer suit.

'You've done well for yourself since you parted company with my father. I heard you got second place in this year's French Grand Prix. Congratulations.'

'Thank you. Your father celebrated

with us afterwards,' he remarked, holding her gaze. 'It was just like the old days.'

'What's the point in dragging up the past, Josef?' she enquired caustically.

'It would make things a lot easier if you and I were friends again.'

'Why? Four years ago we said everything there was to be said. You got your ring back and I've got on with my life.'

'So it appears.' Josef glanced towards the lounge door. 'Is the man who answered the door just a casual acquaintance?'

'Josef, it really is none of your business! I'm no longer your fiancée so I don't have to defend my actions to you.'

'I see the years haven't mellowed your temper, Liebling.'

Instead of telling him that he was one of the few people to be able to rile her like this, she gave an angry snort then demanded, 'Why have you come here, other than to annoy me?'

'I thought I was doing you a favour, Andrea.' He set down his barely-touched drink and stood up. 'Obviously I was wrong. So I'll leave you and your friend to get on with whatever you were doing when I arrived.'

His sarcasm touched a nerve. How dare Josef question her morals when his were virtually non-existent! Andrea got to her feet and put her hands on her hips.

'For goodness' sake, Josef, spit it out! Why are you here?'

'So you and I can clear the air in private.' He seemed to tower over her. 'I'm sure you wouldn't want your father to hear us.'

'My dad?' She pulled away as he reached out to stroke her hair.

'If you go and get dressed, I'll drive you to his office. We can talk in my car. I wouldn't want your friend to overhear us.'

'Dave isn't in the habit of eavesdropping . . . ' She frowned as a thought struck her. 'What are you doing going to the factory?'

Turning on her heels, Andrea hurried from the room. She was twenty-four now and Josef wouldn't find her as gullible.

He had used her to get what he wanted — the coveted seat in Thompson's second car for his first season in Formula One. Josef was a very shrewd man, she considered as she pulled out her blue suit and white blouse, so no doubt this morning's little chat would be to assist him to further his career.

Andrea took her time getting ready, applying a small amount of make-up before slipping on a pair of black court shoes and grabbing a matching bag. Then she headed carefully down the stairs.

'I'm off to work now,' Dave said meeting her by the front door and smiling as he cast an appreciative gaze over her stylish appearance. 'I'm doing spaghetti tonight so do you want me to make enough for you?'

'Thanks but I'm not sure what my dad has planned. He was tight-lipped on the phone yesterday so I don't know if he's arranged lunch.'

'You can tell me about it all later,' Dave whispered, jerking his head towards the lounge door.

'If I must,' she said with a grin.

When Dave had closed the front door behind him, she took a deep breath for courage and strolled with feigned nonchalance into the room.

'I'm ready to go now,' she proclaimed.

Josef was studying the framed sketches in pastels of local scenes on the wall. He glanced over his shoulder.

'Are these all your work?'

'They're old pieces. I don't have much spare time these days to get out and about with my easel.' She glanced at her wristwatch. 'It's half past eight. My father expects punctuality, even from his family.'

As Josef got behind the steering-wheel, Andrea caught the faint hint of his favourite aftershave in the confined space of the sports car. Memories from the past began to flood back into her consciousness but she fought against them.

'Is this your car?' she asked when they pulled slowly away from the kerb.

Josef shook his head curtly but didn't take his eyes from the country lane.

'I picked it up this morning when I landed at Heathrow. My assistant arranged the rental last week along with my hotel booking.'

Her eyebrows drew together. This trip had been planned for days yet her father hadn't bothered to inform her.

'It's nice to be the last one to know — again!'

'There had to be secrecy over this visit, as you'll find out shortly. I asked your father not to inform you of my arrival because I knew you'd have suddenly gone missing.' He glanced momentarily over at her, a smile playing on his lips. 'Your absence in the pit lane has been noted, Andrea. I'm surprised you've never managed to even make the Grand Prix at Silverstone.'

'I don't share my family's enthusiasm for the sport and I have better things to do on a Sunday afternoon than get soaking wet at a noisy track.'

She hoped she sounded convincing. Until her romantic fiasco with Josef, she had adored the nomadic life, flying away for week-ends to European destinations that her friends only dreamed of, to cheer on her father's team from the grandstand. A thought suddenly struck her.

'Who gave you my address?'

'I have my sources.' Josef's smile broadened.

Andrea ignored his cryptic comment, although she suspected she had her mother to thank.

'So you must be keeping up fairly well with my dad's affairs, are you?'

'I'm in tune with the pit lane gossip, that's all. Of course most of it is just talk but when the same thing is being repeated by varying sources, you begin to wonder whether it's not unfounded. I've come to find out how much is true.'

'Someone has been saying things about my father?'

'As I've said, Liebling, a lot of lies are told,' he replied grimly, not returning her gaze. 'It could be that someone is hoping to discredit your father.'

'What's been said?' she demanded, now feeling a bit tense.

'I will tell you later. I don't want you to go into the office, guns blazing!' His gaze met hers fleetingly. 'At times you tend to become hysterical, Andrea. I want you to act rationally today. I believe your father needs our assistance and I'm willing to help so long as you and I can form a united front.'

She wanted to tell him that he had been the one to blame for their break-up. She had heard and seen enough evidence to know she was being used. Their engagement hadn't meant a thing to the Austrian with the roving eye and in a fit of temper she had sent the ring back to him but she had never regretted her decision. No woman would ever be able to tie down Josef Meyer.

'What do you want me to do?' she enquired grudgingly.

'Listen to what we have to say and think carefully before you jump in to air your views.'

'You really think you know me well!' she bit out.

'I learned a fair amount in twelve months, Andrea.' He nodded slowly. 'Do you remember that long, lazy week-end in the Cotswolds?'

It wasn't something she could easily forget. During the wonderful, candlelit dinner in the quaint, centuries-old grey stone restaurant, Josef had asked her to marry him. The following morning they had driven to a larger nearby town where he immediately chose a diamond and sapphire cluster for her.

His arm had gone around her shoulders as the jeweller took the ring from the display case and passed it over. Josef slid the ring over her finger and smiled lovingly down at her.

'Its stones are as bright as your eyes, Liebling,' he murmured then turning to the man added, 'We'll take it.'

That glorious moment had stayed with her for the five months she wore his ring. When she became aware of his infidelity, it was a painful reminder of what she thought he'd felt on that day. All it had been was a stage prop to assist in the charade that he was serious about his love for his boss's only daughter. Weeks after it had been returned to him, there was an announcement in the Press that Josef had signed a contract with the high-ranking Italian team.

Josef's voice cut through her reverie.

'I still have the sketch you did of me that afternoon by the stream. Many people have admired it and have asked me who the artist was. They say you captured my very essence, whatever that means.'

'I didn't consider it to be one of my better ones,' she replied indifferently.

'You shouldn't waste your talent. You're a good artist, Andrea. You should be working in your own studio instead of spending your days at a word processor.'

'Money may not be a problem for you now, Josef, but I have bills to pay each month. If you're not aware, unknown artists don't make much and I don't fancy living on the breadline for the sake of my art.'

'Where are you working at the moment?' Josef asked, turning down the lane which led to her father's business premises.

'You mean my mum didn't tell you?' She chuckled and shook her head. 'I'm the personal assistant for the marketing manager of a local firm.'

'And how have you explained your absence today?'

'I phoned my boss at home yesterday. I told him I was taking a day's leave because of some family troubles.'

'You certainly weren't wrong there,' Josef retorted immediately, stopping the car by the entrance gates of the fenced premises. When the security guard approached, Josef lowered his window and gave his name. 'Mr Thompson is expecting us,' he added. After parking and locking the car, Josef came around and joined her, sliding his arm through hers.

'Remember what I said, Andrea. Think, don't speak.'

Her narrowed eyes met his challengingly though he just grinned and ushered her to the entrance which bore the family's racing logo on its glass doors.

The receptionist smiled warmly at them as they came through the doors.

'Your father is in his office, Miss Thompson.'

Her father gave a beaming smile when they entered his open door and got up from his desk to greet them.

'Andy, I'm glad you've come,' he said, hugging her. 'Your mother and I don't see nearly enough of you.'

As he smiled down at her, Andrea noticed how tired he appeared beneath his healthy tan. His grey eyes lacked their usual sparkle and instinctively she knew something was indeed wrong.

'Did you two meet outside?' her father enquired, returning to his seat and watching their expressions as he did so.

'I gave Andrea a lift. It was on my way from the airport.'

Diplomatically, her father didn't mention the fact that her village was a giant detour from Heathrow. Instead he declared, 'Your uncle won't be joining us this morning. He's had to go to London on sponsorship business.'

Just then, his secretary brought in a coffee tray and set it down on the table before leaving, closing the door firmly her. Her father relaxed back in his chair.

'What we spoke of over the phone, Jo, has now been agreed by the rest of the board. There's one final voice to be heard though, which is why I've asked you to join us today, Andy.' He looked directly at her. 'I'm asking for your support on this although I know you mightn't find it easy, considering what's happened.'

'Go on,' she prompted, whilst pouring coffee for everyone.

'We've asked Josef to sign with us for the next two seasons. How do you feel about it?'

2

Sensing that two pairs of eyes were studying her intently for her reaction, Andrea stared into the depths of her coffee. She longed to leap up and demand why her father should consider Josef for the team when he'd acted so badly towards her, but she stayed where she was.

Trying hard not to openly betray her emotions on her face, she recalled what Josef had hinted at during their drive here. Her father was in trouble and they had to help him. For her parents' peace of mind, she had to forget temporarily the heartache Josef had caused, as difficult as that may become.

Looking up, she regarded each man in turn then replied, 'Our relationship was over long ago. If you want to employ his services then it's up to you, Dad. Josef is an excellent racer and I'm pleased for you that he's going to sign.'

'It hasn't been agreed yet,' Josef cut in. 'There's a lot to consider before the contract is signed. I've got the option to stay on in Italy for another year. I have to know that this move is the right one.'

She sipped her coffee and the cup chinked noisily as she set it down again. Only her trembling hands were displaying her inner fury which she was desperately holding at bay. Images of the stunning, long-legged brunette with her arms around Josef's neck kept flashing into her mind.

'Is there anything else you want me to say?' she enquired, staring between the two men then shrugging as casually as she could. 'You have my blessing.'

'I must say, Andy, I was expecting you to be rather less compliant today.' Her father sighed with relief. 'It won't be easy for you if Josef joins us.'

'Why?' she retaliated sharply. 'I have nothing to do with your business. We won't meet unless Mum invites us to the same dinner parties — which I know she's more than likely to do. But maybe she'll eventually realise Josef and I no longer have any feelings towards one another.'

Josef had got up from his chair to refill his cup so she couldn't see his expression though she heard his slight grunt of displeasure from behind her. Had she gone too far?

'As your daughter seems to accept the situation, Roy, perhaps we should go over everything in detail now? I want to come to a decision within the next few days,' Josef said and returned to his seat.

Knowing what they'd be discussing would be of a highly-confidential nature, Andrea excused herself before they had a chance to ask her to leave the room. She decided to wander down to the factory floor. Music was blaring as the engineers and mechanics worked in their stark, sterile surroundings.

'Andy?' an older man in overalls queried coming from his workbench to meet her. 'Is it really you?'

'I haven't changed that much, Vic.' She shook his outstretched hand.

'Even to an old man, the chassis work still looks pretty good! From a tomboy in jeans, you've grown into a proper woman. Your dad must be proud of you.'

Andrea pointed to the pair of gleaming racing cars standing side by side in the centre of the floor and smiled.

'They're what he's proud of, Vic.' She strolled towards the vehicles with Vic beside her. 'Without them, his life would be empty.'

Stretching out, she stroked the polished black bodywork and sighed.

'That's my phone. I'll be back in a jiffy,' Vic declared, scuttling over to his work area.

Andrea walked around and glanced into the narrow cockpit with its intricate dials, wondering how Josef, just under six foot in height, could squeeze into such a tiny space and perform so well on the track. She fought against her memories but they refused to be abated.

*　*　*

It had been a day just like this. She had been summoned to the factory to assist with some public relations work which had to be completed urgently. Having just left secretarial college and not yet having secured a full-time job, she was glad of any work her father could give her.

During the morning coffee break, she'd come out to the floor to stretch her legs and chat with the men. She had been admiring their latest redesigned car which one of them was polishing in readiness for that day's Press launch. Within days its picture would feature in magazines around the world and she smiled, noticing the loving care the mechanic was taking.

The smile was still on her lips when a hand touched her shoulder and she turned to find her father standing there with a stranger.

'So this is where you've got to!' her dad chided teasingly. 'Andy, this is Josef Meyer from Austria. Josef, my daughter, Andrea.'

He stepped forward, holding out his hand to her.

'I am pleased to meet you, Fräulein Thompson.' His touch was warm when his fingers enveloped hers and she felt as if she'd received a jolt of electricity.

'Likewise,' she murmured unsteadily as his gaze continued to hold hers before it travelled lazily to her lips.

Regaining her composure, she stood aside. Judging from his athletic body beneath the tight jeans and the skin-hugging T-shirt under the unzipped leather bomber jacket, he had to be one of the new drivers her father was considering employing.

'You must be interested to see the new chassis,' her father said and walked on yet Josef remained and smiled at her.

'I already like what I see.'

Blushing profusely, Andrea hurried

back to her typewriter though she was unable to forget the gorgeous Austrian. She was stunned to find him standing in front of her desk two hours later.

'Your father has said you'll know the best place to go for lunch locally and as he's tied up in a meeting, he's given you permission to accompany me.'

'But I've got all this to do and — '

'I'm a stranger in your country, Fräulein,' he said, perching on the edge of her desk so they were perilously close. 'My English isn't very good.'

Andrea smiled wryly and retorted, 'It sounds pretty good to me, Josef!'

Getting her handbag from her bottom drawer, she didn't have second thoughts about joining him.

★   ★   ★

'Dreaming again?'

Andrea started at her father's nearby declaration and spun around.

'I'm always amazed by the in-car technology,' she said, explaining away her surprise at his arrival. 'Where's Josef?'

'He's calling his agent in Innsbruck from my office.' He lowered his voice. 'He seems pretty keen to sign.'

'It's OK, Dad. You have my word that I won't mess up your negotiations.'

'Josef is one of the best, darling. If things were different I wouldn't have put you through this. I know how much you loved him.'

'Dad, as you're always telling me — business is business.' Andrea sighed.

'But not when my daughter's happiness suffers because of it.'

'I can live with it,' she insisted. 'There won't be any ugly scenes. I promise.'

'I really don't know where you get your fiery temper from.' He chuckled. 'Your stubbornness, of course, comes from your mother. Speaking of Moira, she's insisted you're to join us for dinner tonight.'

'Don't tell me — her excuse is that she hates having an uneven number at the table.' Andrea raised her eyes to the ceiling.

'If you mean has Jo been invited — yes, and he's accepted.'

'All right.' She sighed resignedly. 'Tell her she's got her way just this once.'

When she got back to her father's office, Josef had finished making his call.

'I'll drive you home, Andrea,' he declared as they walked in the door.

'Your mother will be expecting you at seven,' her father said as Andrea kissed him goodbye on the cheek.

She walked alongside Josef out to his car in silence.

'So you've agreed to participate in tonight's festivities?' Josef asked lightly, as he locked his seat belt and turning the ignition key.

Looking across at him through now misty eyes, she nodded then thought deeply for a few moments before blurting out, 'Please, Josef, what's going on?'

They had reached the gates and after

waving to the guard, Josef turned right down the lane, the opposite direction from which they'd come that morning. A tear had trickled down Andrea's cheek. She wiped it away with quaking fingers. Josef glanced over.

'I know where we can talk. It looks as if you might need something stronger than coffee.'

She chewed her bottom lip to stop herself crying but when it didn't work, she drew a tissue from her bag and only looked up when Josef stopped the car. They were in the carpark of the pub which Andrea had brought him to five years ago. Her emotions were see-sawing so violently that she suddenly burst into loud sobs.

'It's OK,' Josef reassured her, putting his arm around her shoulders. 'Let it all out. Trust me, you'll feel better.'

Turning her head into his shoulder, she let herself be comforted by him until her sobs subsided into mere gasps for air.

'Are you OK now?' he asked, tilting

up her chin to face him.

Getting a freshly-laundered handkerchief from his jacket pocket, he shook it open and handed it to her.

'Thank you,' she said, moving away from him to dry her face.

'When did you last see your father, Andrea?'

'About two months ago. He's been busy with the European races and when I've been over to the house on the alternate week-ends, he's either been in meetings with prospective sponsors or is at the factory. He's aged since then.'

'I was stunned, too, when we met at the last race. He's not the man I used to know.' Reaching over, Josef wiped a blonde lock of hair that was sticking to her cheek. 'How about that drink?'

Getting out the small mirror from her bag Andrea studied her blotchy face, wishing she had brought her powder compact to hide her red nose.

'I can't go in there in this state. I look dreadful,' she said.

'From what I can remember it's very

dark inside and if you hurry through to the rear tables, nobody will notice.'

While Josef locked the doors, Andrea inhaled the chilly, October air then followed him inside, striding purposefully to the darkest corner as Josef placed their order at the polished oak bar.

'This will go to my head,' she murmured when he set a glass of brandy in front of her.

Sipping the neat spirit tentatively, it stung her throat as it went down and she coughed, unaccustomed to its strength. Drawing his chair closer to hers, Josef spoke in a low voice.

'If you're feeling up to it now. I'll tell you what I've heard.'

Andrea nodded and he went on, 'Several weeks ago I heard rumours that there was some trouble at Thompson Racing. At that point, it was nothing definite, then at the last race I learned it was to do with money. Some of the company's sponsors are becoming rather worried. Apparently two of them are considering pulling out next season.'

'The company will go under!' Andrea's eyes widened in horror. 'Dad and Uncle Tony can't afford to run it without the financial backing of the large corporations. It takes millions of pounds to run a team.'

'So you do know a little about how things work,' Josef declared.

'Of course I do. It was all Dad talked about when I was growing up. It was his passion. Oh, Josef, what's going to happen? The team's his life.'

'I know,' he said flatly.

Andrea was shocked when Josef's hand covered hers on the table and gave it a squeeze. Its warmth was unnerving as was his closeness to her.

'If anyone can help him, it's you, Andrea.'

'Me?' She stared at him. 'He won't discuss the business with me and it'll be rather obvious if I start asking questions after all these years.'

'The general impression seems to be

that not all the money is going to where it should be going.'

'Are you telling me my father is stealing from his own company?'

Immediately she leaped up from her chair though Josef quickly caught her arm and drew her back on to the cushion with a jolt.

'Listen, Andrea,' Josef hissed, still gripping her tightly. 'Someone is playing around with Thompson's finances and your father knows about it. You saw how he looked today — he's a worried man. Why do you think I agreed to come over and discuss terms with him?'

'You mean you've led him on?' She glowered at him. 'You have no intention of returning to his team, have you?'

'What sort of man do you take me for?' he snapped. 'Andrea, your father gave me my shot at racing in the Formula series even though I didn't have as much personal backing as the other likely candidates. I'll always be grateful to him for that. There was no animosity when I left the team. He understood and accepted my reasons for moving on to a larger team. If I can, I'd like to repay the kindness he showed me. From what he's told me, he could be on to a winner with the new design so long as the company is still solvent next March.'

'My dad isn't a thief, Josef. If he's undercharged for something, he'll admit it rather than pocket the money which isn't rightfully his.'

'But somehow we have to find out what's troubling him before it's too late.'

During the drive to her house they barely spoke over the music coming from the radio. When Josef suggested picking Andrea up that evening at six-thirty, she didn't bother to argue that it'd be easier for her to drive herself there. Within hours it felt as though her life had plummeted to hitherto unknown depths of despair.

Even the break-up with Josef was mild in comparison to this. Going to her bedroom, she threw off her clothes and lay on the bed sobbing, wishing she could wave a magic wand so her dad was back to his old self once again.

That evening she was dressed early. The long soak in the bath hadn't mellowed her anger which was directed at the unknown person who was causing her father so much grief.

'What's going on?' Dave asked as she poured herself a glass of lemonade in the kitchen to quench her parched mouth.

'There are a few family problems which I'd rather not discuss at the moment,' she replied, sliding on to a tall stool and watching Dave while he stirred the bolognese sauce. 'That smells good. I wish I was staying in tonight.'

'Is he someone special?' Dave noticed she was dressed smartly.

'I'm going over to my parents for the evening.'

'You don't usually go to such lengths for them, Andy.' He raised an eyebrow.

'Are you sure it's not to do with your earlier visitor?'

'And I thought male house-mates would be less nosy than female ones!'

'Oh, come on. Anyone would be curious why a famous racing driver has arrived unexpectedly on their doorstep.'

'The truth is, he's my ex-fiancé. We split up four years ago and there's not a lot more to add.' Shrugging her shoulders, she sipped her drink.

'You're kidding! All the hours we've spent together and you've never mentioned his name. You're a dark horse, Andy!' Dave chuckled.

'I want you to promise me that you won't mention it to Mick. It'll spread around the village like wildfire and it's something I'd prefer was kept quiet.'

'Josef must have hurt you a lot.' Dave pursed his lips thoughtfully.

'Yes, Dave, he did.'

'And you're still in love with him?'

'Are you mad? I fell out of love with him when he . . . never mind what he did. I know the real Josef Meyer now and I'm fully aware what he's capable of. There's no way I'd succumb to his charms again.'

'You're dressed to kill for a night in with your folks then?' he queried.

Just then, the front door knocker rapped.

'Have a good time,' Dave called to her as she headed for the door, collecting her black, woollen coat and handbag on the way.

As she opened the door, she gave Josef a smile then struggled to get into her coat. For some strange reason, she was suddenly all fingers and thumbs.

'Let me help you,' he drawled, stepping inside and taking the coat so she could slide her arms into the sleeves.

The faint aroma of his aftershave and freshly-washed hair invaded her senses when he brought the material around to envelop her. The gesture was unnervingly sensual. Quickly she stepped away from his body.

'Mmm, that smells very good. What's

cooking?' Josef remarked.

'If we weren't going to Mum's, we could have had some. Dave always makes far too much sauce.'

'Shall we go?' From Josef's cold tone, she knew he was unhappy about something though she couldn't understand his sudden mood swing.

'You look very beautiful tonight, Andrea,' he remarked, starting up the car.

She was glad of the darkness inside the car so her rapidly flushing cheeks weren't visible to him.

'Thank you,' she murmured.

If it had been the old days, she'd have returned his flattery without worry. Instead, she remained quiet even though he did look absolutely stunning tonight in his casual, dark grey trousers, white polo shirt and black blazer.

'So, the man you live with doesn't mind me taking you out tonight?' he asked when they'd been driving for five minutes in an uneasy silence.

Immediately she realised why Josef

was irked. It was fine for him to go out with any woman when he saw fit, yet after four years' absence he'd expected her to still be waiting for him! Deciding to bend the truth a little to protect herself and to deflate Josef's growing ego, she replied, 'I've explained everything to Dave. He knows it's a business dinner.'

'Are you happy with him?'

'Yes,' she answered honestly. 'He makes me laugh a lot.'

'And I didn't?' he countered icily as they stopped at a set of red traffic lights.

'I'm not saying that, Josef. The relationship we had was very different.'

'From what I remember, it was very good.'

As the lights turned to green he accelerated away so forcefully Andrea was thrown back into the leather seat.

'Time can play strange tricks on one's memory, Josef.'

All she could remember was the pain on hearing that woman's voice on the phone at his house in Austria thousands of miles away from her.

'Jo's upstairs,' the woman with the English accent had told her. 'Is it important?'

'This is Andrea Thompson. He was expecting me to call several hours ago.'

She had only just returned home from the wedding reception of her best friend and had called, dying to hear his voice again.

'To whom am I talking?'

'A friend of his.' The woman chuckled. 'He's, er, rather tired at the moment so can I pass on a message?'

'Please, just get him for me.' Andrea's temper was rising rapidly.

'Why are you deluding yourself, Miss Thompson?' the silky voice murmured. 'You must know why he's keeping you sweet.'

'Who are you?' Andrea demanded ferociously.

The woman ignored her question, continuing, 'Miss Thompson, you must be the only person who doesn't know the games Jo's been playing. You're just wearing his ring so his future is guaranteed at your father's company.'

'No! You're wrong!'

'Am I? I'm the one who's here with Jo tonight, not you.'

With that, the distant receiver was put down. Absolutely stunned by the woman's words, Andrea waited for a few minutes before dialling his number. Every ten minutes, for the next three hours, she redialled only to be greeted by the engaged tone.

The seeds of suspicion had been sown. When they next met, Josef denied that there were any other women in his life, but Andrea refused to believe him. Their arguments became a frequent occurrence and when he asked her to accompany him to the end of season Grand Prix in both Japan and Australia, she made an excuse to stay at home.

He didn't really want her there and judging by the later photo in a racing magazine, which showed an attractive brunette with her arms slung around

Josef's neck at a post-race party in Adelaide, she knew their relationship was definitely over. While the vision of the brunette was fresh in her mind, Andrea packaged up the engagement ring, sending it back to him with the terse covering note, *Goodbye, Andrea*.

She suddenly noticed they had arrived at her parents' house and, sensing Josef's gaze was upon her, she confronted him.

'For my dad's sake I'll be pleasant towards you but don't expect me ever to forgive you, Josef!'

3

Andrea reached for the car door handle in the darkness but she was drawn back by Josef's tight grip on her right arm.

'And what do you mean by that remark?' he queried in astonishment.

'We're supposed to be finding out what trouble my dad's in, not going over what went wrong between us.'

Josef shook his head as he took the keys from the ignition, muttering a few words in his native German tongue then adding, 'I don't think I'll ever understand women!'

'We're certainly not as devious as men,' she retaliated, her eyes narrowing.

'Aren't you?' Grinning, he jerked his thumb towards her mother who was waiting by the opened front door and waving at them. 'Tonight we'll see just how manipulative your own sex can be, Liebling.'

When they got out of the car, Andrea's mother hurried to greet them.

'You've arrived together,' Moira Thompson said when she hugged her daughter. 'Isn't that nice?' she remarked happily, turning to embrace Josef.

Over the woman's shoulder, he winked at Andrea. She tried hard not to laugh. Her mum was incorrigible.

'I offered to drive Andrea here so she could enjoy the splendid wine which your husband always serves at your dinner parties.'

'You're still not drinking, Jo?'

'Not while I'm following my strict training régime,' he replied, linking arms with both women and guiding them into the house. 'There are two races to go before I can let my hair down and enjoy the pleasures which have been forbidden during the season.'

'After we spoke last week, I remembered to buy that mineral water you used to like.' Her mum pushed them towards the lounge. 'Go and make yourselves at home. Roy is changing and I've got to see to the main course. Andrea, will you please look after our guest?'

'She'll never change,' Andrea said quietly, watching her mother head for the kitchen. 'I'll pour the drinks.'

Letting him settle on the sofa, she prepared their drinks at the bar then bringing them back, purposely sat in the armchair farthest away from Josef.

'I won't bite you, Andrea,' he mocked, leaning forward to get his glass.

'I didn't want Mum getting the wrong idea,' she whispered, sipping her gin and tonic.

'It mightn't be a bad thing if she does.' He patted the cushion next to him. 'Come over here so she doesn't hear us.'

From his insistence, she knew he'd had an idea so she didn't question whether he had any ulterior motives.

'What is it?' she asked, sitting beside him.

'How much do they know about your relationship with Dave?'

'They've met him and know he's one of my friends.'

'And that's all? They don't know the rest?'

'No.' Her pride stopped her from telling him the truth about her platonic friendship with Dave and Mick.

'Good.' He slid his arm easily across her shoulder. 'Why not let them think that a reconciliation between us may be imminent?'

'They'd never believe it! I can't lie to my parents, Josef.'

'Do you want to help Roy?'

'Don't ask silly questions — of course I do!'

'Andrea, if you and I are a couple, it will seem perfectly natural when you accompany me to the factory. You know many people there. You may be able to find out something from them.'

'There has to be another way,' she contended, trying to ignore the sensations his touch was having on her.

'You can't bear to be with me, is that it?' The chill had returned to his Austrian lilt.

'I have a full-time job and the hours are the same as I was working at Dad's factory. Even if you said you could only visit at week-ends for your seat-fittings, most of the staff wouldn't be there.'

They heard her mother's voice addressing them and just as she entered the room, Josef withdrew his arm from her shoulders. From the glint in her mother's eyes, Andrea knew that she'd already seen. Now there would be no stopping her attempts at matchmaking.

'Has Andrea been looking after you?' Moira asked, sitting down in her favourite armchair. She glanced around as her husband entered the lounge. 'Dinner will be ready in five minutes, dear.'

Andrea noticed her mother's expression change to one of concern.

'I didn't see you in Estoril, Moira,' Josef cut in. 'Were you with your sister back at the hotel?'

'We were in the grandstand as usual,' her mother replied, reaching for her glass of wine. 'I was too tired to go to the pit garage after the race. The previous day we had spent hours going around the shops in Lisbon. That reminds me.' She leaped up from her seat and hurried outside, returning with a carrier bag which she handed to Andrea. 'This is for you — it'll suit you perfectly.'

'Oh, Mum,' she said, taking out and holding up the sapphire-blue woollen dress. 'You shouldn't have!'

'Call it an early birthday present, dear,' she said when Andrea stood up to kiss her cheek. 'When I saw it in the boutique window, I knew it was made for you. Now the cold nights are drawing in, perhaps you'll be able to wear it for a special occasion.'

'The office dinner isn't until December but I think I'll keep it for then,' Andrea retorted, pretending not to understand the nuance in her mother's tone.

'How's the job going, Andy?' her father enquired.

'Same as ever. The boss gives me the mundane reports to do while he keeps the interesting bits for himself. I wouldn't mind but he takes the glory from our directors for anything I do, but when things occasionally go wrong whom does he blame? Me!' She was startled by the sudden peal of laughter beside her and she turned to confront Josef. 'What's so funny?' she demanded.

'I'm surprised you're still being employed by him. No doubt you've given him a piece of your mind, Andrea.'

'I would but my job's on the line. It's not easy finding another job with a secure company. So many have gone under in the past year.' Realising she was stepping on dangerous ground, she continued, 'But when I do find another position and I have his written reference in my hand, then I'll tell him exactly what I think of his underhand methods!'

'That sounds like my daughter all right.' Roy chuckled as his wife came in to tell them that dinner was on the table . . .

'Where are you living now, Jo?' her mother enquired when the plates had been cleared and they were having a respite before their dessert.

'In Austria. I sold my house and I've moved to the next village — St Pieter.'

'What about Monte Carlo?' Andrea interceded.

'I'm perfectly happy where I am on my mountain. I enjoy the solitude after the hectic race week-ends. I don't really need to see the other drivers.'

'What's your home like, Jo?' her mother pressed on.

Andrea watched him while he spoke of the chalet. It sounded idyllic — the sort of place they had decided they would love to share one day.

'This will be my first Christmas there,' he declared, leaning forward to retrieve his glass. 'I've planned to hold a house-warming party on Christmas

Day.' Pausing, Josef glanced around the table and smiled at them. 'If you can make it, you'll be very welcome.'

'Thank you but we can't.' Roy smiled gratefully.

'Isn't the factory closed for the holidays?'

'Yes, for ten days, though that's not the issue, Jo. The family will be expecting us to hold the usual Christmas lunch.'

'No, they won't,' her mother cut in. 'Sharon's baby is due the following week so they'll all be spending the day with Celia and Tony because it's closer to the hospital if she goes into labour early. I'm sure I've already told you, dear.'

'Besides,' Roy went on, 'I doubt we'll find hotel rooms. Austria is popular, particularly over Christmas and New Year.'

Josef turned to him as he got up to refill everyone's glasses.

'I thought you realised that I meant you would be staying in my home. There are plenty of rooms for everyone.'

Tom stopped behind Andrea, putting a comforting hand on her shoulder.

'Andy only gets a short break from work and it wouldn't be fair to leave her to spend Christmas in England alone. I truly appreciate your kind offer, Jo.'

Leaning across, he topped up her glass with wine and again she was struck by the lines of exhaustion etched on his face.

How she wished she could take extra time off so her father could get the break he seemed so desperately in need of. As usual, her boss had beaten her to it and had already booked his holiday dates with the personnel department.

Her mother quickly changed the subject on to that of Josef's family and Andrea was surprised to find out that his married sister now had two children.

'Hasn't Gretchen settled down?'

His attractive younger sister was the same age as herself and four years ago Gretchen had had a string of men at her beck and call.

'I doubt she ever will,' Josef replied with humour in his voice. 'Much to the annoyance of my parents.'

'Mothers do worry about their daughters, even though they claim to be independent,' Moira remarked, staring in Andrea's direction to emphasise her point.

'Shall I bring in dessert, Mum?'

'Don't change the subject!' Moira Thompson stood up. 'I'll get it. One of these days, you'll be sorry you didn't listen to me, Andrea.'

'I'm perfectly happy as I am, Mum. I know you're longing to have a brood of grandchildren but I have to consider what I want from life.'

'And what's that?'

Josef's question caught her off guard. For a few moments she was utterly lost for words. Her mother had stopped at the door to hear her answer.

'Firstly, I'd like to find a job I really enjoy, where I didn't have a lazy boss.'

'It'd be a well-paid one, no doubt?' A smile played on Josef's lips.

'I can dream, can't I?' she challenged him. 'We're talking about the future.'

'How much do you make now, Andrea?'

'That's a rather impertinent question!'

'OK, let's say you've found a job with excellent prospects and a salary which is double your current one. Then what?'

'I'd like to have time off to devote to my painting.'

'You have it. What else?'

'All right, one day I'd like to have children, that's if I met a man whom I loved and trusted.' Blushing from her soul-bearing, she stared down at her lap.

'The job is yours, Andrea,' Josef proclaimed. 'That's if you want it.'

'What do you mean?' She now dared to confront him.

'I was telling your father today that my Personal Assistant is leaving and I've been searching for a suitable replacement. I would expect you to work odd hours because my business doesn't run strictly from nine to five, but you would be given time off during slack periods.'

'I'll help you with dessert, Moira,' her father suggested, ushering his wife from the room before she could object.

'Is this a joke, Josef?' Andrea hissed over the table.

'Not at all. The job is very real as is the salary. I'll double what you're currently being paid.'

She picked up her glass of wine and took a mouthful. This was madness! As wonderful as it might seem in theory, in practice she'd be working for the man who had used her.

'Think before you give me your answer.' Josef leaned towards her, adding quietly, 'You wanted an excuse to be at the factory more often and I've handed it to you. You'd be based in Austria and I'd want you to accompany me on my overseas trips to handle my business while I'm concentrating on my racing.'

'You don't know what I'm like at

work,' she protested. 'Plus I only know a bit of German which I learned from you.'

'I know you well enough to know how you throw yourself into everything enthusiastically. Most of my contacts are English-speaking though I'm sure you'd soon pick up the necessary German phrases for answering the telephone. If you can keep your temper under control, I'm sure things will work out.'

During dessert and coffee, the topic wasn't mentioned so Andrea was certain her father had warned her mother not to interfere. From her mother's taut expression, it was clear she was itching to ask if Andrea had accepted.

At ten-thirty, Andrea decided it was time they were leaving.

'I've got to get up early tomorrow for work,' she explained when her mum tried to persuade them to stay and have another coffee. Catching sight of her father's ashen features, she knew what she had to do. 'For once, I'm looking forward to it.'

She smiled at Josef who helped her on with her coat.

'I hope you'll change your mind about Christmas, Dad, because by then I'm going to be in Austria with Josef.'

★   ★   ★

'It has certainly been a strange day,' Josef remarked when they'd been driving for a short while.

'That's an understatement if ever I heard one,' Andrea said, her voice not echoing his amusement.

'I take it you're having second thoughts?'

'It's a bit late for that. I've just announced it to my parents. Mum will already be planning what to pack for the trip at Christmas.'

'I did warn you not to be impetuous.'

'What option did I have, Josef? In front of them you offered me precisely what I'd said I was looking for.'

'You could have said you would consider it for a few days.'

'We're not all as perfect as you, Josef.' She crossed her arms indignantly. 'I wish I could think before I act but however much I try, I still jump in.'

'You possess some admirable qualities, Andrea. You will fight for what you believe in and you have the utmost loyalty to your family. As for myself, I'm not perfect by any means. I've made some serious errors of judgement in the past.'

In the darkness, Andrea stared down at her ringless finger, swallowing deeply. Obviously their engagement had been one of them.

'You'll find out when we get to Austria,' he continued, 'that I'm dreadful at keeping up with my paperwork so don't take any excuses I may come up with for avoiding it. After a month or so, you'll be used to the routine.'

'Will you be arranging somewhere for me to live in the village?'

'You'll be living with me.'

'What?' she stormed turning to look at him.

'I thought I made it clear that I'd need you to live on the premises. If I've spent the day training at the gym, we may have to work until the early hours.'

'No problem. I'll take my car over there,' she insisted.

'It won't make a lot of difference. As you'll have to give at least one month's notice, you won't be starting for me until early December — about the time when the first snow of winter will be falling. The track down to the village can be treacherous. Even with chains on the tyres of the four-wheel drive, I wouldn't tackle it at night unless there was an emergency.'

'Then it must be bad,' she murmured.

There were few things Josef wouldn't attempt — he had the spirit of adventure and was willing to try anything at least once, no matter the danger involved.

'You'll be taking over the quarters

which my current assistant will be vacating. They're self-contained within the house. Outside of working hours, you'll have as little or as much contact with me as you wish.' He slowed as they approached her village. 'I'll leave you my hotel number in case there's anything else you need to know. I'll be there until Wednesday morning.'

As he pulled up in front of her house, he turned off the engine straight away. For once, the place was in darkness.

'How are you going to break it to Dave?' Josef asked.

Andrea's whole body tensed.

'I'm sure he'll understand when I tell him I'm doing this for my father.'

'This will be a new career for you, Andrea. We're not talking about a temporary position. I need someone I can depend upon to run my affairs in my absence.'

'I thought you meant I was only staying on until my father's company was out of trouble.'

'I don't recall saying anything like

that in our negotiations.'

'If you had, I'd have thought twice, Josef!'

'You have several options.' Holding out his hand, he ticked off his fingers in turn as he spoke. 'You can tell your parents you've changed your mind and neither you nor your father will hear from me again. Or you can take the permanent position I'm offering and I will not only sign with his company but I will assist you in any way that I can. Then there's the last option.' He glanced up at her. Instantly she felt cold as his tongue traced over his bottom lip.

'Which is?' she enquired hesitantly, shuddering as his arm came behind her seat and his hand brushed her shoulder.

'You can stay with your boyfriend and at your current place of employment. I will sign the contract if you act as if we are a couple when we're in company. It may be fun, though not necessarily the best one to clear your father's name.'

'That's blackmail!'

'Call it what you will but I'm a businessman, Andrea. I want to help because of my loyalty to Roy — one which you and I share. Why do you think I came here?'

'Because he asked you?'

'No. I contacted him and enquired what the chances would be of me racing for him next season.' His admission shocked Andrea. She thought Josef Meyer only considered himself, no-one else.

'If I sign, I want to be pretty certain that his team will be racing next season. I'm prepared to take the risk by leaving my current team who pay me an excellent salary, so what are you willing to do for Roy?'

'I'm really tired, Josef. I'm not thinking straight,' Andrea said, rubbing her temple with her fingers hoping to ease the beginnings of a headache.

He handed her a card bearing a hotel's name and telephone number.

'I have your home phone number so I will call you tomorrow night at eight o'clock. By then, you may have realised there is only one route we can take.'

'But can you guarantee this will work?'

'I'm not a fortune-teller, Andrea. If the worst comes to the worst, at least we can say we've tried.'

'I'll talk to you tomorrow, Josef.' Andrea sighed heavily.

'Sleep well,' he murmured in German as she opened the door and stepped out into the cold night air. Hurrying up the path, she dug into her deep pockets for her keys, knowing all the while Josef was watching her from the car. Her hands trembled as she fitted the key into the lock. After a perfunctory wave towards him, she closed the door behind her then waited with baited breath until she heard the car start up and move off.

She was startled when a figure came down the darkened stairs. Quickly she turned on the hall light.

'I hope I didn't disturb you, Dave.'

'I was awake. I'd just turned my lamp off before I heard the car pull up. You look as if you've got the world's troubles on your shoulders tonight. Do you want to talk, Andy?'

Nodding, she got up and closed the door so they wouldn't disturb Mick.

'I could do with talking a few things over if you don't mind.

★ ★ ★

The next day at work, she had to stifle her yawns as she sat in a meeting with the department heads. She and Dave had talked over endless cups of tea, until the facts and Josef's list of options were spinning around in her head.

'You're not really with us today, Andrea, are you?' her boss joked rather pointedly just when the clock hands indicated the working day was over.

Her sapphire eyes narrowed though she swallowed her terse reply. Instead, she got up from her desk and put on her coat.

'Where are you going? That report is due on Thursday,' he stormed.

'My hours are nine to five-thirty. It will be completed in the morning.'

'But I need to make my own additions tomorrow!' her boss declared, sounding a bit like a petulant child. 'This really isn't good enough, Andrea. With barely any notice, I let you have the day off yesterday.'

'Good-night,' she remarked sweetly, picking up her handbag and heading for the lifts. She may have discounted Josef's third option in the early hours, yet she wanted to break the news to her boss at the right moment and when she was certain Josef would keep to his word.

Dave had prepared dinner for the two of them as Mick was working late.

'The time won't go any faster if you're continually watching the clock,' he said, getting up to make a pot of tea. 'Ring him if you're that desperate, Andy.'

She shook her head, remembering the last time she had phoned Josef and his female friend had answered.

'I don't want him to know how much I'm depending on his help.'

'I wish there was something I could do,' Dave told her over his shoulder. 'I'll be here if you ever need me.'

When the phone rang, one minute after eight, Dave answered the kitchen extension as they'd planned, to give Andrea moments to compose herself.

'Well, have you made a decision?' Josef's deep voice came down the line.

'Yes, Josef. I have.'

4

Taking a deep breath before continuing, Andrea prayed she was making the right decision. It was as right as it could be, given her limited options.

'Send me a contract of employment, Josef, and I'll sign it.'

'It will be delivered within the hour.' With that, the line went dead.

'I don't believe that man!' she said, slamming down the receiver. 'He was so sure I would sign, he's already had a contract drawn up!'

'You have to face facts, Andy. He knew last night what your answer would be. The only thing holding you back was your pride. Most people would kill for such a high-powered job. I'd love it if I had your training.' He chuckled. 'Living in Austria, travelling the world and staying in the best hotels. It beats working as a cook in a steamy kitchen any day!'

'I'm really going to miss you and Mick.' She gave him a big hug.

'We'll miss you, too, though we'll be here if you need us.'

When the knock came at the door, Dave tactfully took himself upstairs.

Andrea was surprised to find a strange man standing there.

'Fräulein Thompson?' he enquired. Seeing her nod, he went on. 'I am Erich Stoll, Herr Meyer's personal assistant. May I come in?'

While she carefully read through the contract, which had been drawn up in German with an English translation, the man got out a sheaf of papers and put them in order on her coffee table. Over the next two hours, the man informed her of the work she'd be expected to do and of the arrangements for her move from England, which he would begin to put into action the following day.

'Do you mind if I ask you why you're leaving your job?'

'I am getting married in January, Fräulein,' he said. 'Although I would like to continue working for Herr Meyer, it wouldn't be a good way to start married life. The working hours are very erratic, as you will find, but he's a good employer. I have agreed to stay on while you settle in. I have also agreed to spend an hour with you each day teaching you the German language, Fräulein.'

'As it seems we're going to be together a lot, Erich, perhaps you should forget the formalities and call me Andrea.'

★   ★   ★

During the next five weeks, Erich was on the phone to Andrea a lot, keeping her abreast of the arrangements, even when he was in Japan and Australia while Josef was racing there.

Her boss wasn't at all pleased when she handed in her resignation but she ignored his cutting remarks and let the office gossips do her dirty work. In no time, everyone in the firm was aware of her new position and on the whole they were full of congratulations and encouragement.

In the lounge with Dave and Mick, that evening, she watched the recorded highlights of the final two races on the television. Her father's team didn't do well in either of them, causing the commentator to air his opinion on the surprise pit lane news that Josef Meyer would be racing for the small British team next season.

'He's kept his side of the bargain,' Dave whispered to her.

Andrea visited her parents on their return and noted her father still looked exhausted beneath his now darker tan, though she did get him to agree to the Christmas trip.

The last days sped by alarmingly. Most of her belongings had been transported and her old room seemed bare. The rest she would either be taking with her on the plane or would be stored in the house's loft until she gave Dave further instructions.

Erich arrived in a hired car to collect her for her flight. Tearfully she hugged her two friends when they'd stored her cases in the boot.

'We have to go, Fräulein, or we'll miss our slot,' Erich told her.

Through her tears, she tried to reassure herself that what she was doing was right, yet there were still nagging doubts in her mind. All the way to Luton airport, she was deep in concentration so she was very surprised when they arrived there but didn't pull up outside the entrance to the regular terminal building.

In minutes, a porter had taken her luggage and she was ushered with the utmost speed across the Tarmac to a waiting executive jet. Its engines began to rev as she and Erich were climbing its short flight of steps.

'This is unbelievable!' she whispered on seeing the sumptuous decor of the aircraft. It was like no plane she'd ever been on. There weren't formal rows of hard upright seats but huge comfortable-looking armchairs separated by tables on either side of the centre aisle.

'Please, follow me,' Erich said to her. 'We will be leaving in five minutes as the slot we have been given for take-off is eleven o'clock.'

She did as she was asked, staring in amazement while they passed down to the chairs towards the back of the cabin. Erich was now indicating to two seats with an outstretched hand. When she stepped forward, she stopped abruptly.

'What are you doing here?' she stammered in surprise.

Josef got up from his rear-facing seat and smiled.

'And a good morning to you, too, Fräulein Thompson,' he replied before handing out an order to Erich who hurried back down the aisle. 'I had some unfinished business in England and I thought it would be pleasant to have some company to while away the hours on my return journey.'

Sitting down, she secured her seat belt then glowered across at him.

'I'm your new assistant, Josef. Nothing more.'

'It doesn't mean that we can't be cordial with one another, Andrea.'

'So long as that's all it is,' she muttered, staring out of the small window at the drizzly view when the plane began to taxi towards the runway.

She gripped the arms of her seat as they were finally propelled into the air. They were buffeted until the plane had cleared the rain clouds and she was relieved when the seat belt sign was turned off.

'Coffee, tea or something stronger?' Josef enquired.

'I'm OK for the moment, thank you.'

Even though Andrea was a seasoned flyer, she felt as though she'd left her stomach behind. She was positive it had something to do with her travelling companion. She hadn't seen him, other than on television, since the night of her parents' dinner party. How she hated admitting to herself that even after everything he had done, she was still attracted to the man. But her father's future was what she had to concentrate on.

'I was sorry to hear your car let you down in Japan,' she remarked without rancour as Erich brought a bottle of mineral water and two glasses to their table.

'It happens.' Josef shrugged, thanking him. 'You can go back to your book, Erich, but don't tell me the ending because I want to borrow it from you afterwards.'

'You actually make time to read these days?' she parried.

'My life has changed. The months you and I spent together were — what's the word? — intense. We lived each moment as though it would be our last,' he said, filling their glasses. Josef held her gaze as he handed hers over and their fingers brushed. 'We couldn't continue like that. Something had to give.'

The truth was he had become bored with her and had sought out a more interesting woman to share his precious moments with, she considered silently.

'Did you learn anything new while you were overseas?' she asked quietly, uncertain of where Erich was doing his reading.

'Not much. A few people asked me if I was making the right decision and I told them I was. Perhaps it will temporarily halt the pit gossip. I know your father was approached in Adelaide by a major company over a deal for next season because one of their top men wanted my assurance that I had signed the contract with Roy's team.'

'Do you think we could be wrong, Josef? Somebody might be spreading around all these rumours hoping to discredit him and my uncle. We don't know they're true.'

'You have seen your father with your own eyes and have remarked on the change in him. In the past, he has defended his team vehemently. It is his silence which is worrying me, Andrea.'

On arriving at Innsbruck airport, their luggage was soon bundled into Erich's estate car and Andrea was pleased to find the first snows hadn't yet arrived.

The valley they drove along, swamped on either side by towering mountains, was delightful in the early afternoon sunlight.

Leaving the motorway, they drove up a road which wound through dark pines.

'We'll soon be there,' Josef informed her, turning around in his seat while Erich continued to drive carefully.

An ornately-carved wooden sign announced they were arriving in St Pieter. Andrea's eyes widened as they entered the main street of the tiny village. Either side of them stood ancient buildings with shutters and sloping roofs, just like those in the illustrations of the book of Grimm's Fairytales she used to have.

At the end of the built-up area, between two fields, they turned on to an even smaller track. They climbed higher and higher. Andrea's heart was in her mouth upon noticing the sudden drops by the side of the road. 'Way down below them was the village where the parked cars now looked like miniatures.

'Here we are,' Josef proclaimed, and she turned her attention forwards to find they were entering a set of high gates.

Her nervousness was increasing. She was being stranded in the middle of nowhere — alone — with Josef! Inwardly she cursed herself for being so trusting.

'Come along inside. Your luggage will be taken to your quarters where your other things are,' Josef said, taking her arm in his and guiding her to the entrance of the building which she was staring at with incredulity.

Although the sprawling chalet was obviously very new, it had been built in the old style with dark, wooden shutters at the windows. The front door opened and an elderly woman stood there, trying to keep hold of the collars of the two eager dogs either side of her. Nearing the woman, Josef said something and she let them go. Immediately the Labradors came bounding towards Josef and greeted him eagerly.

'You're frightened by them?' Josef asked with concern when Andrea stepped back several paces.

'No. I was just trying to get out of their way!' she replied, smiling.

'The black one is Donner and the golden one is — '

'Blitzen?'

'Correct.' Josef grinned. 'They are aptly named. Like thunder and lightning, these two can create much havoc.' He gave an order and immediately the dogs headed indoors. Leading her over to the woman, he stopped. 'Fräulein Thompson is my new assistant. Andrea, this is Frau Unger, my housekeeper and cook.'

'Welcome, Miss Thompson,' she said, smiling and holding out her hand towards Andrea who shook it. 'I speak only a little English, Fräulein.'

Josef put his arm around Andrea's shoulder as he replied to the woman in German before turning to translate it for Andrea.

'I said that soon you would be speaking our language like a native so her morning coffee breaks will become more enjoyable.'

'You've got more faith in my learning abilities than I have!'

'We'll see who's right in a few weeks,' he replied, ushering Andrea inside. 'Frau Unger will show you to your quarters so you can freshen up then I will join you in the dining-room for a late lunch.'

There were several doors leading from the large entrance area and Frau Unger opened one for her, announcing, 'The dining-room.'

As the woman bustled along the hallways, Andrea was trying to remember which turns to take by the pictures hanging on the wall at crucial intersections.

Eventually the woman opened a door, letting Andrea go inside ahead of her.

'Your rooms,' she said with a smile.

They were in a small lounge, decorated tastefully in warm hues, which had its own armchairs, television and stereo system. Then Andrea followed Frau Unger into the next one. In the centre was a carved, wooden, queen-size bed, covered with an attractive handmade quilt.

The other pieces of furniture were of the same dark wood. Mahogany, Andrea guessed, suddenly wondering why there were no wardrobes. The answer soon became clear — off her private bathroom was a dressing-room which had plenty of storage space and several full-length mirrors. Her boxes and cases were stacked along one wall and one of her first tasks would be to unpack them all.

'This is wonderful,' Andrea exclaimed.

'Your rooms are OK?' Josef asked

later as Andrea joined him and Erich at the table in the dining-room.

'They're very nice, thank you,' she replied.

Frau Unger came into the room bearing a huge platter of assorted cold meats, cheeses, pickles and salad. Erich held out a basket of freshly-cut, home-baked bread for Andrea and she took a piece, finding it was still warm.

'Erich will be helping me this afternoon,' Josef informed her as they started on their meal. 'No doubt you'll be needing a few days to get acclimatised to life here and to unpack the many things you've brought with you.'

Across the table, Andrea saw the corners of his mouth twitch as he held back his amusement so she quickly jumped to her own defence.

'My luggage comprises mostly of warm clothes for your notorious climate.' She tugged at her blouse's tight neckline as she was unused to such an efficient central heating system. 'Maybe I should have purchased things for the tropics instead of getting thermal wear and thick jumpers.'

'We don't stand on ceremony in this house, even during working hours, Andrea,' Josef declared in a more serious tone. 'You can wear what you like here, though when we are travelling I will expect you to dress in a suit.'

After the meal, Josef and Erich headed for the study so Andrea returned to her room to settle in. That evening she dined alone. Frau Unger brought her meal to the table in Andrea's lounge.

'Where is Herr Meyer?' Andrea enquired when the woman set it down.

The woman thought carefully for a minute then uttered in hesitant English, 'He's busy tonight. He's gone out, OK?'

Andrea returned the woman's beaming smile, adding, 'I understand.'

Her smile vanished as soon as the woman did. She suddenly felt so lonely and was irked that Josef had left her alone on her first night in the country.

It was silly, she thought, while picking at the tasty pork cutlet and vegetables, because she had been the one who wanted to keep a distance between them and now she was annoyed at getting her own way.

Sleeping fitfully in the strange bed, she awoke early still feeling gloomy although her mood changed as she threw open her bedroom curtains and was confronted by one of the most glorious sights. Quickly pulling on her wrap to cover her nightie and stepping into her mule slippers, she unlocked and opened the picture windows. The morning air was crisp but she stifled her shivers to step on to the wooden veranda for a better view of the valley. Going to the railing, she smiled. It was so beautiful.

A voice in the distance called her name and she glanced around in surprise. Josef was in the meadow below the house and he waved to her as his two dogs continued to sniff at every blade of grass. She returned his wave then hurried inside, wondering how long he'd been watching her.

'You should be more careful,' he taunted her when she arrived in the dining-room for breakfast, joining him at the table.

'I couldn't resist it,' she confessed. 'I had to get a better view of the mountains.'

'So long as you don't make it a habit, Andrea,' he replied. 'You'll be having the local men waiting every morning to catch a glimpse of the fair maiden.'

'It won't be happening again!'

His humour, at her expense, annoyed her.

'What you do in your own quarters is up to you,' he said warmly. 'This is your home, too, now, Andrea. I wouldn't dream of trying to stop you from doing anything you want — within reason.'

'I don't think so,' she murmured, trying to stop her lips forming into a smile. 'I'd rather build on having a good reputation around here.'

At that moment Erich came into the

room and Josef's attitude towards her changed. They spoke about what work would have to be achieved that day and as Andrea had finished her unpacking she insisted on joining Erich in the office.

The morning passed quickly. She watched as Erich took dictation then was shown around by him while Josef worked out in the gym. Andrea was getting her bearings when they returned to the main lounge for coffee.

'Does Josef go into the village to train?' she enquired when Erich was pouring out their drinks from the coffee pot Frau Unger had brought in.

'You remember the farthest door at the pool?'

He came over to her armchair and handed her a cup.

'Yes, I do.'

The indoor pool and adjoining Jacuzzi had come as a surprise to her. She'd been glad to learn she could use them in her spare time.

'It leads to his private gymnasium.

His personal trainer comes most days and Josef will inform you at his morning briefing of the times he will be unavailable. He hates being disturbed in there so do your best to put off any callers. Most of his friends and business acquaintances know of this so they'll ring back later.'

'Does he entertain here often?' she enquired lightly then sipped her drink. 'It's a large place for a man on his own.'

'It's not my place to comment on my employer's private affairs, Miss Thompson, and I'd urge you to remember the clause in your contract regarding secrecy.' Erich was choosing his words with care.

'Sorry, Erich! I was just asking you to satisfy my own curiosity.'

His gaze went from her face to a point over her shoulder. She turned in her chair to see what he was looking at. It was Josef's sketch portrait which had been framed and was hanging above the oak and stone fireplace.

'It's a very good likeness, don't you think?'

Andrea got up and strolled over to it, annoyed that tears were pricking the corners of her eyes. It was far better than she'd remembered. It was as if a stranger had done the picture of Josef. The planes of his handsome face were strong and true, and there was a force behind his amber-brown gaze.

'It's so passionate, so alive,' Erich was saying and she was only half-listening to him. 'How strange,' he remarked suddenly, causing her to spin around. 'I hadn't noticed this before. It has been signed by someone with the same initials as yourself — A.H.T.' The man's dark eyes were dancing as he regarded her expression and she felt he knew the truth behind her recent bout of nosiness. 'That's quite a coincidence, wouldn't you say, Andrea?'

5

It's wonderful to see you,' her father said as he greeted them on their arrival at the English test track which his team used. 'How are you getting on?'

'Very well,' Andrea replied as he slipped his arm around her shoulders and they walked away from the pit garage.

'You can speak truthfully. Josef has gone inside to change.'

'I mean it, Dad.' She smiled at him. 'I might only have been there just over a week, but I'm liking it. The house is fantastic and Mum will love it when you come for Christmas. The scenery is — '

'Andy,' he said, pulling her to a stop and getting her to face him directly. He looked concerned. 'Why did you accept Josef's offer?'

'Because it was too good to pass up.'

She stared into his grey eyes, hoping he'd believe her. 'Although I've got Erich's assistance at the moment, I know I'm going to get on well. I have quite a lot of free time. If I'm not walking the dogs, I go on to the mountain and sketch.'

'He's already broken your heart once.'

'Dad, I was still a teenager and I didn't know what real love was,' she insisted with fervour. 'I haven't gone to Austria hoping to pick up where our relationship ended. Josef and I rarely meet outside of working hours. I have more contact with Erich who's trying hard to teach me German.'

She had been quietly proud of her achievement in so short a time.

'Is he having much success?'

Before she could reply, the tranquillity of the countryside was shattered by the sound of a car's powerful engine being revved up nearby. Quickly they both covered their ears with their hands. She walked back to the garage with her father where she was handed a pair of snug-fitting earphones by one of the mechanics. Josef smiled at her when he came into the garage, resplendent in his black and silver driving suit, the colours of the team.

Standing against the wall, so she wasn't in the mechanics' way as they worked preparing the vehicle for Josef's first drive in it, she watched as he tugged on his flameproof headgear and adjusted the eye holes. Over the raucous din, her father and Josef were holding an animated conversation. With a final nod, Josef put on his distinctive helmet then slid gracefully into the narrow cockpit.

While a mechanic strapped him in, Andrea went outside to the railings by the track where her father was standing. Together they watched as he drove the car slowly out of the garage towards the pit lane exit.

'This is a splendid day for me,' her father remarked when they were finally able to speak and gave her a tight hug.

'I never thought I'd see Jo wearing the team colours again. Isn't this like the old days, Andy?'

Rather too much, she thought wryly, pursing her lips. Only today she wouldn't be greeting Josef with his usual kiss in the garage. She winced as the roar of the V10 engine approached them down the straight and it passed feet away in a flash.

'It's a miracle!' her father exclaimed when they heard Josef was bringing in the car.

Seeing that his expression was the happiest it had been recently, she nodded emphatically.

When Josef was in the debriefing with her father and the race engineer, Andrea chatted to the men while they were having a well-earned tea break.

'Will we be seeing you at Estoril in January, Andy?' Vic enquired.

'It's highly likely now I'm Josef's assistant.'

'I'd heard rumours,' Vic countered. 'You know what this place is like.'

'Most pit lane rumours are totally unfounded but in this instance, it's true,' she said, watching his expression which didn't change.

'Well, I must get on, Andy.'

She managed to chat to two others though was unable to turn the conversation in the direction she wanted. Either they were being purposely evasive or were innocent of what was happening.

With the test being declared a success, they returned to the factory where Josef had his first seat fitting. Again she phoned Erich and took down an urgent message to pass to Josef when the men had taken a mould of his body so that for next season he'd have a perfectly-fitting seat.

'Anything?' Josef asked on rejoining her and taking the note from her grasp.

'No, absolutely nothing,' she replied with a sigh.

'Don't worry, it's early days.' Josef patted her shoulders.

Back in Austria, Andrea found Frau

Unger was busy with the preparations for Christmas, now only a week away. Her parents were arriving on Christmas Eve morning and she realised she hadn't yet bought their gifts. So, during one of their slack periods, Andrea went with Erich to a nearby town to purchase presents for them and some boxes of chocolates for Josef's family.

'I think I've finally got everything,' she beamed, coming out of one last shop and letting him take some of her many carrier bags.

Over the next few days, Andrea kept looking expectantly out of the window for snow. Her excitement was growing now she had wrapped her presents. She'd been uncertain whether to buy something for Josef in town. She didn't want him to get the wrong idea about her feelings towards him yet she didn't want to exclude him as he'd been so courteous since her arrival in Austria.

He was a man who had everything he needed, so privately she had done a sketch of the house from the meadow and today had asked Erich to pick up a ready-made frame while he was in town on an errand for Josef.

Sitting alone in the office during Erich's absence, she stared out and watched the approaching clouds with interest. Was that a fleck of snow which just passed the window? She got up from her chair and muttered a curse as the ringing phone stopped her from investigating further.

'Guten morgen,' she said politely on picking up the receiver then added in English, 'This is Herr Meyer's residence.'

'May I speak to Josef Meyer?' a woman's voice enquired.

Josef was in his gym and she heeded Erich's warning that he hated being disturbed.

'I'm sorry but he's busy at the moment. Can I help you? I'm Andrea Thompson, his personal assistant.

'No, I have to speak to Herr Meyer,' the woman insisted in perfect English. 'This is a private matter.'

A cold chill trickled down Andrea's spine and she stiffened.

'If you leave your number, I'll get him to call you as soon as he's free.'

'He has my number. Please tell him that Helene called. Thank you.'

As Andrea put down the phone, her hands were trembling. Why was the woman being so enigmatic? Turning, she should have been delighted to find that snow was falling quite heavily but instead she felt strangely empty.

It was going to happen sooner or later, she reasoned, strolling to the window and resting her forehead against the pane. Josef was an attractive man and she doubted he'd lived like a monk since they'd parted. Even she'd had a few dates though she hadn't been very interested in men. Maybe she should have got on with her life instead of comparing them all to Josef.

She sighed deeply.

'A penny for them,' a deep voice declared behind her, making her jump.

'I was watching the snow falling,' she

replied, blushing under Josef's scrutiny. 'Isn't it wonderful?'

'In days you will be bored with it.' He chuckled, wiping his face with the towel slung around his neck. 'Before I shower, are there any messages?'

She steeled herself for her reply, trying hard to keep her tone noncommittal so he wouldn't think she sounded even slightly jealous, because she wasn't.

'A woman called Helene phoned you. She said you have her number.'

'Excellent. I'll call her from my room so I don't disturb your work.'

As he closed the door behind him, she let out an exasperated sigh.

Although she woke early on the morning of Christmas Eve, she found Josef had already left for Munich airport to meet her parents' flight.

As Frau Unger continued with her cooking, Andrea got on with the task of decorating the five-foot sapling pine which had been brought in the day before. Its resinous aroma was permeating the warm room and having found the coldest place to position it, she began to trim it with tinsel and the delightful hand-carved wooden toys. Sitting back on her heels, she smiled, admiring her work.

Suddenly she was aware of Donner and Blitzen barking eagerly at the front door and she got up, hurrying to join them. Josef parked the vehicle as near to the entrance as possible and she waited until her parents were inside the house before hugging them.

'I'm so pleased you're here,' she said, tears trickling down her cheeks.

'Come into the lounge and get warm,' Josef declared as Frau Unger took their snow-flecked coats.

'Did you have a good journey?' Andrea enquired.

'We landed on time and thankfully this country is geared up for snow. The roads were clear apart from the one leading up here,' her father said, grinning at his wife. 'Have you got your stomach back yet, dear?'

'I'd hate to think what it'll be like if it continues to snow,' Moira Thompson remarked. 'We mightn't get back to England until spring!'

'Don't worry abut the return trip.' Josef laughed. 'If we're snowed in, you'll be able to get down to the village in the gondola lift.' He had strolled to the window and was pointing. 'The middle station is just over there.'

'A lift?' Moira gasped, not sharing his humour. 'I hate heights, Jo!'

'He's teasing you, Mum,' Andrea said, taking a glass of Glüwein from the tray Frau Unger had brought in.

'Willkommen, Fröhliche Weihnachten!' Josef raised his glass to them.

'Merry Christmas,' they all echoed, sipping the spiced, warmed, red wine.

'This is lovely,' Moira remarked, taking a larger mouthful.

'It's also very potent, Mum, so beware.' Andrea glanced over at Josef. 'Can I show Mum around?'

'Of course,' he replied cordially. 'You know which room will be theirs.'

Andrea's mother was visibly impressed by what she saw.

'This is wonderful!' Moira enthused as they arrived by the indoor pool. Steam was rising from its azure water. 'I can understand why you sounded so happy in your letters, dear.' Confronting Andrea, she took her hand and squeezed it. 'It's not just the place though, is it?'

'Mum!' She sighed. 'I'm Josef's employee — nothing else.'

'Not yet maybe.'

'Never, Mum! We have a good working relationship and that's all. I don't want you reading more into it.'

'Then why did Jo offer you the job? He wanted the opportunity to get back together with you, of course.'

'My experience had something to do with it. I'm trained for the job and I've been brought up in the world of Formula One so I'm not daunted by his celebrity status nor the circle he moves in.'

'But aren't you hoping your relationship

might blossom again? You two are so right for one another.'

Linking arms, Andrea led the way back to the lounge.

'It was never meant to be. Please, Mum, let's drop the subject.'

After lunch, the four of them dressed in warm clothes and took the dogs for a walk across the snowy meadow with Andrea keeping her mum chatting while Josef walked ahead with her father. She doubted her dad would speak openly about his worries yet it might help him to know Josef was willing to listen to him.

Frau Unger joined them for dinner then Andrea and Moira insisted on helping her load the dishwasher. Considering neither of the older women shared a common language, they got along surprisingly well and sent Andrea back to the lounge to rejoin the men who were discussing the recent test drive.

'Dad, you should forget the business for now,' she chided lovingly as she sat beside him on the sofa. 'This is Christmas. You should be unwinding.'

'It was my fault,' Josef cut in. 'I promise it won't be mentioned again during the holiday.' Getting up, he poured out glasses of brandy and brought them over. 'Are you excited yet, Andrea?' he asked, handing one to her.

'Most people feel sorry for me seeing as my birthday falls on Christmas Day but I think I'm lucky,' she replied, taking her glass and smiling.

'Has she been peeking at her presents?' her father enquired.

'Not while I've been watching.' Josef chuckled. 'Though you and I may have to stand guard over them tonight.'

'I can be very patient!' Andrea contended. 'If you don't believe me, I'll wait until your family gets here tomorrow to open mine.'

'We'll hold you to that but you'll be regretting your words in the morning.'

How she hated it that Josef knew so much about her! Why couldn't he just forget everything he'd learned like she'd tried to do?

The time would soon arrive when she'd find out that she'd been omitted from Josef's list. Though why was she letting it get to her? As she'd told her mum, there was nothing between them and what she hadn't said was she was here to clear her father's name.

*   *   *

Early the next morning, she threw open her windows. To her delight, the church bells were pealing in the valley. Dressing quickly, she went to the dining-room where Josef was finishing his breakfast.

'Happy birthday,' he said warmly as she sat opposite him.

He poured coffee from the pot into a cup and passed it to her.

'Were you on the early-morning shift guarding my presents?'

'I trust you implicitly, Andrea,' he replied, his eyes gleaming. 'I know when you give someone your word, you won't go back on it. I'm going to church soon. Would you like to join me?'

'Em ... What about my parents? They'll wonder where we've gone.'

'We'll leave them a note. We'll only be gone for an hour and Frau Unger will see to them in the meantime.'

'OK, I'd like that,' she said, tucking into her rolls, smoked ham and cheese.

'I'll see to the dogs and meet you out front in fifteen minutes.'

Josef got up from the table and left the room.

Andrea changed from her casual clothes into her sapphire woollen dress and black knee-length boots before meeting him as arranged. Not having been down to the village since the snow had fallen, she now understood why her mother had been apprehensive though Josef drove slowly and carefully down the track.

During the service, which Andrea couldn't understand because it was conducted entirely in German, she admired the wonderfully decorated church, conscious all the while of Josef's presence beside her.

Outside afterwards, he was greeted by many of the churchgoers and introduced Andrea to them.

'Fröhliche Weihnachten,' she kept repeating in her best accent, wishing she knew what they were all discussing.

'When Erich finishes working for me, I will be taking over your German tuition. By your next birthday, you will be fluent, Andrea.'

Until this moment, she hadn't really considered the ramifications of her career move. Her father's troubles would hopefully be over but she hadn't considered she might still be here next Christmas!

6

You haven't changed a bit, Andrea!'
Josef's mother, Luise, hugged her
warmly then stepped back to admire
her again. 'You're as pretty as ever.'

They strolled to the lounge and
joined the rest of his family and
friends who had arrived. The place was
buzzing with animated conversation
and Andrea's mother was helping Frau
Unger with everyone's drinks.

'So, you're working for my son,'
Luise remarked. 'Is he treating you
well?'

'Very well. I was very pleased when
he offered me the job.'

'He was deeply wounded when you
left him, Andrea.'

Suddenly the day didn't feel quite so
pleasant.

'It was all his doing, Luise. I was hurt
by his deception. He broke my heart.'

'Yet you've come back to him?' There was a wry gleam in the woman's eyes. 'But whatever your reasons, I'm glad you're here with us.'

Over the next half-hour, all the presents were distributed and duly unwrapped until Andrea had a stack of gifts by her armchair. She smiled around the room. 'Thanks everyone. They're marvellous.'

Andrea avoided looking at Josef in case he noticed that her eyes were no longer glinting. She couldn't let him see what he'd done to her. She'd known he wouldn't bother yet it still stung.

'Andrea, could you pop out to the kitchen and help Frau Unger?' Josef asked.

'Yes, of course,' she replied, hiding her inner despondency and threading her way through to the adjacent room, only to find that the kitchen was empty. As she looked out of the side window, wondering where the woman had disappeared to, Andrea heard the kitchen door close. Startled, she spun around.

Josef was standing there, watching her.

'Is something wrong?'

'You asked me to help Frau Unger. But I can't see her anywhere.'

'Because I've just sent her to the dining-room. I wanted a few moments to be alone with you.'

'Then why didn't you say so instead of lying to me?'

She regarded him with caution as he approached her.

'I didn't want our families around when I thanked you for my present, Andrea.' Stopping he smiled down at her. 'It was a lovely surprise and a very unexpected one.' Heat rose to her skin as he bent his head and pecked her on the cheek. 'Thank you.'

'It was nothing.' She shrugged her shoulders in a casual manner.

'You must have spent a lot of time over it and I'm grateful.'

She tried to walk away but he caught

her arm in a vicelike grip.

'Please wait, Andrea.' With his other hand, he drew out a small gift from his jacket pocket and held it out to her. 'Happy birthday.'

Josef let go of her and she undid the small case, gasping on seeing the gold chain and its pendant of an intricately-worked Capricorn goat — her birthsign.

'Let me fasten it for you,' he said, taking it from the cream satin.

Going behind her, he laid the necklace against her neck. She stared down at the piece in stunned silence while he did up its clasp then turned her around so he could view it.

'Very beautiful,' he murmured.

'It is, Josef,' she agreed, amazed as the tiny sapphires and diamonds sparkled up at her.

'I meant you,' he said, tilting her chin upwards with his fingertips. 'You're a very beautiful woman.'

His mouth came down on her lips.

His kiss was everything she remembered but as she fought to escape, his arms enveloped her body and held her tightly to him. She tried to recall the pain he'd caused yet as his kiss intensified in passion, she found herself responding easily to his caresses.

Breaking away for air, she stared into his eyes with horror.

'This can't be happening!' she panted breathlessly. 'You're my boss!'

'Does that matter?' he countered in wry amusement. 'Our relationship doesn't have to stop when work is over.'

'It does. I couldn't stand being hurt a second time!'

'Are you denying you're attracted to me?'

'What woman isn't, Josef? We've been through this before.' Her body quivered as his fingers stroked her face then lightly traced the outline of her lips. 'Please, don't force the issue otherwise I'll have to resign. I couldn't take more of your games.'

'This is no game, Andrea. I am

perfectly serious in my intention. I have been attracted to you for some years and that will never change.' He shrugged. 'If it means getting you up on my mountain out of your lover's clutches, so be it.'

'You might have won me over in the past but I know what you're capable of. I'm not as naïve as I was, Josef. Your women friends are still calling you and you're rushing to be at their side. Please credit me with some intelligence! I had an inkling that my relationship with Dave forced your decision, as my dad's problems later did for me.' Her mouth twisted. 'On the day everything is sorted out, you'll be receiving my resignation in writing as per your contract of employment. Thank you for the gift, Josef.'

Pretending to be happy, she returned to the party in the lounge noticing that Josef didn't rejoin them until some time later.

'That's a beautiful necklace,' Luise said as Andrea topped up her glass of pre-lunch champagne. 'If I'm not mistaken, it's one of Helene's pieces.'

'Helene?'

What on earth was Josef doing giving her jewellery which belonged to another woman?

'She's one of the best craftswomen in the area. Her designs in gold are always distinctive and are highly sought after.' Luise turned over the pendant and smiled. 'Yes, it's one of hers. You're lucky to have been given this.'

Andrea, full of remorse and abject embarrassment, avoided Josef until the others went into the dining-room to help themselves from the buffet tables laden with hot and cold delicacies.

'I'm sorry if I was rude to you earlier,' she whispered, sidling up to him. 'I misinterpreted things and it was a kind gesture on your part, Josef.'

'So now you know who the mystery woman in my life is?' His eyes bore down into hers. 'Who my mystery caller was?'

'Yes.' She nodded apologetically.

'You'll never learn, will you? You jump in, always believing the worst of me.'

For once she bit back the angry retort which immediately sprung to mind regarding his infidelity and she just shrugged. After a few seconds of calming herself, she said in an even voice, 'I'd like to set things straight, Josef. You may be capable of running a professional and personal relationship in tandem though I don't think I could, even if I wanted to. You've hired me to do my job well and that's what I'll be doing. What we had together is in the past.' She took a deep breath. 'You've got what you wanted — I'm up here on your mountain and Dave is back in England.'

'Does that mean we can't be friends?'

'From what happened a short while ago I don't think it'll be possible. You want more than I'm prepared to give, Josef.'

As he stared down at her, she wondered if he could guess how difficult a time she was having, holding her old emotions at bay. Being in his arms had been like returning home. If only she could trust him, she'd have no problem whatsoever adjusting to a relationship which continued after office hours.

'Then why don't we start by calling a truce? I won't make any more passes if you promise to keep your kisses to yourself.'

'You arrogant — '

'What's keeping you two?' Gretchen's voice startled them. Josef's younger sister grinned at them. 'Sorry, did I interrupt an important discussion?'

'You arrived at a fortunate moment,' Josef replied in German. 'My assistant and I were having a minor disagreement.'

'It was hardly minor,' Andrea muttered under her breath.

'Let's go and eat,' Josef said, linking his arm through hers. 'And after the holidays, Andrea, please remind me to congratulate Erich on his coaching. He really has done a great job in a few weeks.' He chuckled. 'I'll have to watch what I'm saying in future, won't I?'

Her feelings of annoyance with Josef gradually evaporated as she ate the delicious meal. Once the buffet was cleared away and coffee was brought around with accompanying glasses of brandy, Andrea was surprised to see her mother coming in from the kitchen with a birthday cake, a single candle burning on the top.

'Don't forget to make a wish,' her mother whispered in her ear.

While everyone sang 'Happy Birthday' Andrea glanced around, smiling. On reaching Josef, she knew she could wish for the impossible, that she could one day trust him. Her gaze travelled onwards until it got to her father's still pale face. Inhaling and wishing hard, she blew out the candle. It would take more than this to help him, but if it stacked things slightly in his favour then why shouldn't she believe miracles might happen?

'You will be coming with us on New Year's Eve, won't you, Andrea?' Luise said while her son helped her on with her coat at the end of the day.

Andrea frowned as she stared at Josef for enlightenment. Josef slid his arm around his mother's shoulders.

'Of course Andrea will be joining us for dinner. I couldn't let my personal assistant see the New Year in alone up here. It wouldn't be very fair, would it?'

Leaning forward, Luise pecked Andrea on the cheek.

'It was good to see you again. You're welcome to drop by the house at any time — you know where we are.'

Andrew nodded but doubted she'd be taking up the invitation. There were too many memories at the Meyer family home — their surprise engagement party which most of the village had attended being one of them.

The rest of the evening passed pleasantly with more glasses of brandy and friendly conversation. It had been one of the best birthdays she'd had and she felt a little sad when her mother began to stifle yawns.

'It's been a long day,' Josef said, rising from his chair. He whistled to his Labradors who were curled around Andrea's ankles like oversized slippers. 'If you don't mind, I'll turn in once I've taken the dogs for their last run.'

'I'm tired, too,' Andrea echoed, feigning a stretch of exhaustion. She was wide awake but if she stayed up she knew her mother would insist on keeping her company, regardless of how tired she was feeling.

After kissing her parents, Andrea returned to her rooms preparing to settle for the night. In her private living-room, having changed into her pyjamas and satin wrap, she sat on the settee and studied her wonderful gifts. There was a bottle of her favourite perfume along with toiletries of the same fragrance from Josef's sisters. His parents had got her a set of oil paints and another of coloured charcoal sticks plus numerous accessories for her hobby.

The gorgeous black gown her own parents had bought was already hanging up in her dressing-room. Fingering her necklace and glancing down at it, she knew she would be wearing the gown on New Year's Eve as its scooped neckline would show off Josef's gift to advantage. She sighed recalling his kiss and the argument which had followed. Why couldn't things ever be simple?

Leaving her presents on the settee, she went to bed hoping that sleep would come even though her brain was alert, rerunning the passionate embrace over and over like a crazed video recorder.

'This is no good,' she mumbled, fumbling for her bedside lamp switch.

Putting on her wrap and slippers, she opened her door and crept towards the kitchen along the silent corridors. A mug of hot milk should do the trick. She stopped dead when she reached the lounge doors. The reading lamp in the corner was still on. Her parents must have forgotten to turn it off, she reasoned, padding across the carpet.

'Andrea?' She turned in amazement at the sound of her father's voice. 'Can't you sleep either?'

'You gave me a start, Dad.'

'Sorry, darling. I was sitting here thinking. I didn't mean to disturb you.'

'I got up for some warm milk. Can I get you some, too?'

Roy picked up the brandy glass from the table beside him and took a sip.

'No, thanks. I'll finish this then join your mother.'

'Why don't you stay here and keep me company?' She smiled sadly at him. 'We haven't had much time alone for ages.'

'That sounds like a good idea.'

Preparing her drink quickly she joined him on the sofa so their conversation could be kept to a low hum.

'Are you happy here, darling?' her

father enquired as she sipped her sweet, warmed milk.

'Yes, I am. It's a lovely place. I have everything I need and I'm enjoying the variety of the job. It's better than being stuck in an office from nine to five.'

'And does your happiness have anything to do with your new employer?'

'Josef and I have mended some bridges. We work well together though there may be a few upsets when Erich leaves permanently. I want to reorganise the office so I know where everything is kept. I also intend to be firmer with my boss.' She chuckled. 'Until now I've been accepting his excuses for putting off dictation and so on, but come the New Year I'll be putting one of my resolutions into practice — to knock him into shape!'

Her father echoed her laughter quietly as he set his empty glass on the table.

'I'll believe that when I see it! Jo's great in a car. He can pinpoint the smallest problem yet trying to get him to sit through a long debriefing after a test is a nightmare.'

'Then why did you renew his contract after his first season with the team?'

'Because he's one of the best, darling. He gives one hundred and ten per cent on the track whether it's racing or testing. Out of the car he needs a little coaxing to stay still for an hour or two. Who knows? If you can get him to toe the line, he might be more compliant with our engineers.'

'Josef has never sat still. He's always on the go.'

'Maybe I'm wrong, darling, but I've seen a change in him recently. Perhaps your influence is already rubbing off on him.'

'I don't think so, Dad.' Andrea shook her head. 'He lives his life to the full. Twenty-four hours in a day have never been enough for him.'

As the words tumbled from her lips, she realised her father might be correct. There had been no wild parties since she'd arrived and his visits to the 'strange' woman had been explained. He'd popped out on several occasions without telling Andrea where he was going but she was just his employee not his keeper.

The old Josef would take off on a whim to visit one of his pals on the other side of Europe. When they'd become engaged, she got used to being given hardly any notice that they were heading off for the beaches of Italy or the slopes of Switzerland. Her life certainly hadn't been dull with him. And it wasn't now. It was less frenetic but still as pleasurable.

'You've gone very quiet, darling.'

'The milk must have started going to work,' she replied gazing across into his concerned expression. Lines of fatigue were etched on his face. 'You should have had some, Dad. You look so tired these days and I'm worried about you. Is something the matter?'

'Big business is taking its toll, that's all. Before the team was set up, I didn't realise what would be involved. Maybe I was too naïve.'

'Dad, it's not as if you've just finished your first racing season, it was your eighth.' Andrea covered his hand with hers.

'There have been a few niggles, though you don't have to worry yourself, darling. Now Jo's back with us, I know the recent bout of bad luck we've been having will pass.'

She wasn't fooled by her father's tone of bravado. Easily she could see through his act and she squeezed his fingers.

'I'm sure it will,' she replied, knowing that's what he wanted to hear.

'Have you finished your drink?'

'Go to bed, Dad. I'll be fine.'

'If you're sure.' Getting to his feet, he leaned across and kissed her on the cheek. 'I hope your birthday wish comes true, darling.'

'Wish?'

'Your birthday cake.' He winked at her. 'It won't be long before you and Jo work things out, birthday wish or not. Sleep well.'

When her father left, she slid her feet from her slippers and brought her knees up to her chest. Hugging them to her, she sighed. She felt so useless! Her father obviously needed help yet he wouldn't burden his family. Didn't he realise that the old saying about a problem being shared becoming a problem halved was in many ways true? At least if he gave someone an inkling of what was wrong, they might be able to point him to the best place to get advice.

Andrea grimaced. Pride was something she and her father shared genetically. Perhaps if she had asked for advice and heeded it when her relationship with Josef was going wrong, it might have been sorted out. Her father never acted as impetuously as herself yet he hated to admit that he'd made a mistake. But what was the mistake? Had he gambled on a project that had backfired?

'Oh, Dad,' she whispered. 'What have you done?'

7

Despite feeling physically and mentally exhausted the next morning, Andrea immediately agreed to Josef's suggestion that she join him skiing.

After a late breakfast, she changed into her navy ski suit, pleased that it still fitted her four years on. Zipping it up, she headed to the lounge to meet Josef.

'Are you sure you'll both be OK while we're out?' she asked her mother and father. 'I feel dreadful leaving you alone.'

'Go on,' her mum insisted. 'You love skiing and this is your first real chance since you've been here. Go and enjoy yourselves.' Her gaze travelled over to Josef. 'We'll take the dogs out in a while then I'll help Frau Unger so that lunch is ready when you return.'

'You're here to relax, Moira,' Josef

reminded her. 'You're my guests.'

'You'd better go,' her dad cut in. 'You'll be here all day trying to dissuade her!'

Within an hour, it seemed as though Andrea hadn't been away from the slopes. Luckily Josef was being patient and waiting for her to catch up with him on the way down to the village. The crisp breeze blew away the cobwebs from her head while she followed in his path.

'That was fabulous!' she said, catching her breath when they reached the lower valley. Framing her eyes from the brilliant sun hanging in the cloudless azure sky, she scanned the mountain for Josef's house. She could just see it.

'Are you ready to walk along to the lift station?'

'Slowly, if you don't mind.' She smiled in reply. 'I should have been exercising in your gym, Josef. I'm out of shape plus it doesn't help that I didn't sleep well last night.'

'Why? Did something happen after I

left you?' Josef asked, watching her while she took off her skis.

She met his amber gaze directly and told him of her talk with her father.

'And that's all he said?' Josef queried as they strolled together.

'I'm positive. He said now you're back with the team, his luck will be changing for the better and I've nothing to worry about.' She stared across at him. 'He didn't convince me, Josef. I've been worried sick all night.'

'Well, they're staying until Tuesday morning. Perhaps when he feels a bit more relaxed he may speak to you again.'

'You know what he's like.' She shook her head. 'He'll bottle it up inside of him. I'm so frightened his health will suffer, Josef. We've already noticed this is taking its toll on him.'

Josef grasped her arm, pulling her to a halt.

'For now, there's nothing more either of us can do other than making sure he knows we're on his side. After New Year you and I will have to work hard to find out the truth, yet I have a suspicion it's not going to be easy, even though we've combined forces.'

'If only he weren't so stubborn, Josef!'

'I'm saying nothing.' He grinned. 'I don't want to get into an argument on this beautiful day about inherent traits.'

'And which side of the family do you get your lack of order from?' she countered while they walked on. Noting him shrug his shoulders, she smiled. 'You do something about your untidiness and I'll try to be less rash and stubborn in the future.'

Stopping at the end of the queue for the gondola lift, Josef held out his gloved hand to her.

'Let's shake on it. We'll see who's first to break their resolution.'

'I know it won't be me,' she responded, shaking his hand and smiling as she noticed his raised eyebrows. 'That's not stubbornness, Josef, but feminine intuition! You'll soon go back to your old ways.'

'Then you don't know me very well, Liebling. When I set my mind to something, I'll see it through to the end.' His expression became serious when he lowered his voice, adding, 'And that applies to finding out what's causing Roy to worry, too.'

★ ★ ★

For the next five days, the atmosphere in the house was one of happiness and fun. At last Andrea was feeling at ease again in Josef's company and between them they were able to raise her father's spirits until he was almost back to his old self.

It was only when they were saying goodbye in the airport terminal on New Year's Eve morning that she noticed his anxiety had returned.

'We'll see you both very soon,' she said, kissing her dad's cheek. Standing back, she looked him in the eye. 'Take care of yourself, Dad.'

'You, too, darling,' he replied, smiling sadly.

She wished she could book a ticket and go home with them. As they said their final goodbyes, she fought back her tears. Once her parents had gone through into the departure lounge, she let go of her emotions and Josef put a comforting arm around her shoulders.

'We'll fly out to England as soon as we can,' he reassured her.

'I feel so useless being here, Josef,' she said when her sobs ceased. 'I might find out more if I was in England.'

'Trust me, Andrea. This is the best way,' he said.

'But — '

'But nothing, Andrea. As hard as it might be, try to put the matter out of your mind. We'll deal with it when the time comes. Besides I need your full concentration today. You and I have a lot to cover.'

'I thought we weren't going to begin work until Thursday.' She had planned to have a leisurely stroll with the dogs and a swim in the pool before getting ready for tonight's dinner with his family.

'We're going to spend the day together but from this moment, every word will be spoken in German.' He opened the car. 'That's the only way you're going to learn the language, Andrea.'

'Josef, this is going to be difficult,' she said, sliding on to her seat and buckling her belt.

'Auf Deutsch, bitte,' he replied starting up the engine.

Getting ready in her room that evening, Andrea realised she still had a long way to go until she'd be fluent. Luckily she wasn't feeling as self-conscious now over her pronunciation. When Josef had corrected her, he hadn't made a fuss about it. Four years ago he'd have been the most unlikely person to have done coaching. Perhaps her father was correct that Josef had changed.

Not outwardly, she considered, as she

met him in the lounge that evening and saw him dressed in an immaculate black suit. Josef smiled on catching sight of her and got up from his chair.

'You look beautiful, Andrea.'

'What happened to the pact of only talking in German?' she jested, taking care in her high heels as she walked across the room to join him.

'Working hours are over. Speak in whatever is easiest for you,' he murmured. His gaze travelled from her carefully blow-dried blonde hair down to his gold necklace at her neck. 'I'm going to be the envy of every man tonight.'

His words made her tremble inside and she was caught unaware from a sudden headiness.

'Won't we be late?' she enquired breathlessly.

'My family is used to my unpunctuality. Why spoil the habit of a lifetime?' he replied, stepping forward towards her then taking her hands in his.

His skin was warm to her touch while

he raised her left hand to his lips and kissed it gently.

'We should go, Josef,' Andrea prompted half-heartedly.

Her brain was saying this was wrong yet the rest of her body was in total disagreement. No other man had ever had this effect upon her. Everything he'd done in the past no longer seemed of importance.

'Maybe we should — my family is expecting us after all.'

Taking his arm, she walked with him to the front door where she changed into her pair of après-ski boots. Most of the paths and roads had been cleared of snow but she didn't fancy ending up with a broken leg for the sake of fashion. Like the others, she would leave her boots with her padded coat in the restaurant's cloakroom for her return journey.

'It's wonderful to see you again,' Luise Meyer remarked, getting up from her chair and kissing Andrea's cheek.

Josef, meanwhile, greeted the rest of

his family who had taken over a long table in the plush hotel's restaurant. Andrea was introduced to several of his aunts whom she hadn't met before and she spoke in German to them without any hesitation. Bottles of champagne were already on the table and as Josef took his seat beside Andrea, he filled her fluted glass then returned the bottle into the ice bucket.

'Aren't you having any?' she asked him.

He called out to a passing waiter and ordered mineral water. Turning back to Andrea, he shook his head.

'Maybe one glass at midnight.' He smiled as he indicated to his parents sitting opposite them. 'They're lucky. They only have a five minute stagger down the road.'

As Josef's gaze met Andrea's, goose pimples erupted on her arms. What was the point in denying this attraction which hadn't diminished since that first day when he'd arrived hoping for a seat with her father's team? They had been close friends, too, which was why his treachery had cut deeply. Over the past week they had joked and chatted like in the old days. If their relationship was meant to be then she had to forgive Josef's indiscretion and look to a future with the man she hadn't stopped loving.

The gala dinner of Austrian specialities seemed endless. Course upon course was served and Andrea could feel her waistline expanding with every mouthful. She sighed thankfully on seeing the coffee pots and cups being delivered to them.

'That was a lovely meal,' Andrea said to his parents. 'Thank you for inviting me.'

'You're welcome,' Luise replied, smiling between Andrea and her son.

It was an expression of hope which Andrea had seen all too often during her own mother's stay at the house.

'I hope you will do me the honour, Andrea, of giving me the first dance when we move into the other room,' his father cut in.

'I'd be delighted, Otto.'

When the coffee was finished, they moved into the ballroom at the rear of the hotel. The head waiter had reserved a huge table for them which was away from the group playing on the stage. Before Andrea could sit down, Otto took her arm and led her to the dance floor. It was a slow waltz and she followed Otto who was a proficient dancer.

'Don't you think you should ask Luise to dance now?' Andrea asked as the next song began.

On their way to the table, Otto met a friend and started chatting to him, so Andrea returned alone. She noticed Josef and his mother were also deep in conversation at another table. Sipping the wine which had been left for her, she began to think of some German pleasantries she could share with his aunts.

A woman's voice nearby cut through

her contemplation. It was an extremely familiar one — but why? After a few moments, she realised the woman was talking in English. Andrea's ears had become accustomed to picking up anything tonight, regardless of the language. Glancing over her shoulder, she didn't recognise the attractive brunette who was talking to an older man. But why was the woman's accent so familiar?

'Sorry we've been so long,' Josef apologised on reaching the table. 'I thought my father was keeping you company.'

'He's met up with people, too. I've been resting after that wonderful dinner.'

'Josef!'

She noted his smile falter for a split-second when the brunette called to him.

'Jo, is it really you?'

They were both amazed by the woman's gushing arrival. The brunette hugged Josef tightly then drew back.

'Hello, Francine,' he replied in a clipped manner, pecking her on the cheek.

'You dreadful man!' Francine slid her arm through Josef's. 'Why didn't you call me?'

An inflection in Francine's voice suddenly brought everything back to Andrea. She stared with animosity at the woman who was all over Josef like a rash. It was her — the woman at his home the night she'd phoned him! A mental picture of the two of them together popped into her head and Andrea couldn't bear to watch them any longer. Snatching up her handbag, she got to her feet. Neither of them would miss her if she went to the cloakroom to calm her rising temper.

'Andrea, come and meet an old friend,' Josef said before she had moved behind the first chair.

Rather than show anything was annoying her, Andrea put on her best smile and joined them.

'Andrea, this is Francine. She's from England, too.'

'Pleased to meet you,' Francine murmured unconvincingly. 'Are you over here on holiday?'

'No, I work in the area.'

'Oh, you're a tourist rep in one of the ski resorts?'

The brunette's hazel eyes quickly passed over the figure-hugging gown, obviously summing up her opposition.

'Andrea is my new assistant,' Josef interceded.

'What's happened to Erich?'

Francine draped her arm around his shoulders. The plain gold band on her finger glistened under the lights.

Should she feel happy that the woman was married? As her composure was about to break, Andrea excused herself and walked with her head held high to the cloakroom. On returning she found the pair had moved on to the crowded floor where they were now embracing under the pretence of a slow dance.

I'm not jealous, she reasoned. Josef was playing his games again. How could she have been so stupid to think he'd changed? At least she hadn't agreed to further their relationship. Her heart might be aching though at least her self-respect was intact.

Wait, an inner voice cried out. Was she leaping to conclusions? Shouldn't she let Josef have his say? The woman was married and the friendship could be just that — a platonic friendship. Finally the music ended and Andrea sighed gratefully as they broke apart and Josef began to chat to someone else.

Francine then returned to the table to collect her brandy glass.

'So, you're Andrea,' she purred after taking a sip of her drink. 'When we were introduced I didn't realise you were Jo's ex. What on earth has brought you back to Austria?'

'Isn't your husband looking for you?' Andrea responded pleasantly.

'He and I have this understanding.

Our marriage is an open one.' The woman's smile was intensifying. 'You must really love Jo to put up with his philandering under your nose.'

'How I feel about Josef, Francine, is none of your business. I'm not questioning your scruples — and you're the one wearing a wedding ring, not me. Josef and I are free agents. We can see whoever we want to.'

'You'll never tie him down, you know.' Francine hissed. 'He's the sort of man who's never satisfied with having only one woman in his life.'

'Then I had better take care when his girlfriends call the house in future.' She didn't feel particularly pleased on seeing Francine's smile disappear but the woman deserved a dose of her own medicine. 'These German names sound so alike to my untrained ears. I wouldn't want him to turn up at Marie's home when it's Maria who's called.'

There was a rustle of ruby satin and

Francine was gone. So were any expectations of a rosy future, Andrea thought grimly.

Five minutes later, Josef came back though by now Andrea was feeling prickly. She longed to confront him to ask him what had happened between himself and Francine, and also whether it was still going on but she didn't dare to in public.

'We haven't danced yet,' Josef remarked. 'It's nearly midnight.'

'These new shoes are killing me,' she fibbed.

'Take them off! I promise not to step on your toes.'

'I'm feeling tired, too.' She took a mouthful of wine.

'Andrea, is something wrong?' he asked, sliding on to the chair opposite hers. 'I'm truly sorry I've left you alone this evening. But I know many people here and it would be rude to ignore them.'

'I'm fine, Josef.'

'Then dance with me, Liebling.'

'Just one or I'll have blisters tomorrow,' she said, getting up and joining him.

Hours earlier she had been longing for the second when he'd put his arms around her and pull her into his firm embrace. Now it was happening, her senses were numbed. Even the sensual aroma of his aftershave couldn't re-ignite her passion. Her heart was heavy as her love for him hadn't decreased.

'What's going on?' he whispered in her ear, causing her to shiver.

'I don't know what you mean,' she countered, continuing to hold him as she would a stranger and deliberately keeping a distance between them.

'Put your arms around my neck, Andrea. I won't bite you!'

'You're my employer, Josef, and I have a reputation to uphold. I don't want people to think we're living together.'

'I hate to remind you, Liebling, but we are.'

'Under the same roof maybe but that's as far as it'll be going.'

'Andrea, will you please tell me what's going on?'

Before she could reply, the band stopped playing abruptly. They turned to see what was happening. The owner of the hotel was on the stage and he began to speak into the microphone, in German.

'Ladies and gentlemen, there is one minute until midnight.'

With Josef's arm around her waist, it seemed like the longest sixty seconds of her life as the crowd counted down to the New Year.

'Funf! Vier! Drei!' everyone chanted together. 'Zwei! Eins!'

The entire room erupted into a mass celebration as the old year ended.

'Happy New Year,' Josef said, bringing Andrea back into his embrace and kissing her on the lips.

'Happy New Year,' she echoed unenthusiastically, pulling away from him.

Josef glowered down at her.

'Tell me, what is going on? I thought things were good between us.'

'I'm sorry if you got the wrong idea but I'm here purely to help my father.'

'I don't believe you.'

She sighed, noticing his parents and sisters were approaching him.

'That's the way it is, Josef.'

Hugging his family and wishing them all the best for the year ahead, Andrea wondered what it was going to hold for herself, Josef and, most importantly, her own parents.

8

And how are things with you, darling?'
her father asked when Andrea phoned
him several days after their return to
England.

'Much the same,' she fibbed down
the line.

Calling the atmosphere between her
and Josef strained was an understatement. Thank heavens he was locked
away in his gym just now with his
trainer. Since leaving the restaurant
within half an hour of the New Year
beginning, Josef had barely spoken to
her. Later today they would be going
through his business for the next month
and she wasn't looking forward to it.

Erich had phoned, saying there was a
hitch with his wedding arrangements
which had to be sorted out immediately
and would Andrea explain to Josef.
She'd been hoping Erich would be here

to ease the atmosphere.

'When will you want Josef over for his final seat fitting?' she asked her father when she'd assured him everyone was fine.

'Is Josef there with you?'

'No, he's training but if you let me know the best dates, I'll get back to you later this afternoon, Dad.'

'We'd like him over within the next few days if it's possible so his car is ready for the testing in Estoril at the end of the month.'

'In that case, I'll make sure I speak to him as soon as he's free.'

After putting down the phone, Andrea felt lonelier than ever before. At least in England she had friends and family she would visit but here she was reliant on Josef, Frau Unger and Erich for company. Just then, the door flew open.

'Are there any messages before I shower?' Josef grunted.

'My dad wants you in England within the next week for the seat fitting.'

'Get Erich to arrange the travel details when he gets in.' He rubbed his damp face with his towel. 'Where is he? It's not like him to be late.'

'He's not coming in until later. There's been a last-minute hitch.'

Andrea steeled herself for an angry outburst but it didn't come.

Instead he walked over to his desk and opened the back page of his large diary. Picking up the phone, he punched in a number. He spoke quickly in German and Andrea was only able to catch the occasional word. When he was finished, he went behind his desk and sat down.

'You can call Roy and tell him we'll be there tomorrow morning. I can only fly over for the day because it's Erich's wedding the day after.'

'It's come around so quickly! It'll be his last day with you tomorrow.'

'And then it'll be just you and me, Liebling,' he replied sardonically.

'It seems a bit mean to leave him alone.'

In truth, she was scared that all responsibility was being passed on to her shoulders. The work didn't bother her, it was whether she'd pass on an incorrect message seeing as her German still wasn't fluent.

'You want to find out what's wrong with your father, don't you? You made it perfectly clear the other evening that's the reason you're staying here.'

'I know, but — '

'Be ready to leave at seven in the morning.' He got to his feet. 'If Erich arrives before I'm ready, tell him I've spoken to the pilot and he's arranging the take-off slot for eight-thirty.' As he went to pass where she was standing, he stopped dead. 'You don't have to worry about Erich's wedding present. I've got one already for them.'

'I hadn't thought about it,' she said, feeling guilty.

'No problem. I'll add your name to the gift tag.'

'You don't have to, Josef.'

'As you'll be going to the wedding as

my partner, it makes sense. I'll be back in half an hour.'

The next day, over in England, Andrea wandered around the factory chatting to some of the mechanics while Josef was having his last fitting completed.

'I bet you can't wait to get to Estoril,' she said to one of the younger ones. 'You might get to see some sunshine.' She hugged herself. 'I hate this English weather — wet and gloomy.'

'I'd heard you were working for Josef in Austria. It must be colder there at the moment.'

'It is, but it's a dry coldness. Over here you feel chilled to the bone from the endless rain and wind.'

'Steven, have you got a minute?' another man called to him.

'Can't it wait? I'm chatting up a gorgeous blonde!'

'No, it can't. I thought you put in the order for those disc pads.'

The mechanic strode over and slammed a sheaf of papers on the bench. Andrea stepped away so as not to get involved. Behind her, the conversation went on. The men spoke in hushed voices though she overheard every word.

'I did,' Steve replied defensively. 'They arrived this morning.'

'Did you check the number that arrived?'

'No. Vic has had me working on this so I thought either he or one of the others would do it.'

'Steven, how many did you order?'

'The amount you asked me to, of course!'

'Then I suggest you ask for a hearing-aid for your next birthday! We're six short and there's a shortfall on other items.'

'I'm telling you I filled out the form like you asked before passing it on to the management for authorisation. I can't understand why we're under again.'

'Again?'

Andrea's ears pricked up.

'I spoke to Vic and he sorted it out with the distributors. They put it down to being understaffed in the warehouse due to the flu that was raging just before Christmas.'

'Steven, please take care next time. This could cause us problems if it happened during the season. Luckily we're not going to Portugal for another three weeks. We could have lost a lot of valuable testing hours there with this shortfall.'

'It won't happen again. I'll make sure of it,' Steve replied.

'It might be better if you kept your mind on the job instead of chatting up any woman who strolls in here!'

Andrea turned around and the older man's jaw dropped.

'Miss Thompson! I didn't know you were here. Aren't you supposed to be in Austria?'

She waved her hand towards the area where Josef was.

'Word spreads quickly, doesn't it?' She smiled pleasantly. 'I'm over on a flying visit. I had a few minutes to myself so I thought I'd catch up on everyone's news.' She turned to Steve, holding out her hand. 'It was nice to meet you, Steve. I'd better go — my boss will be wondering where I've gone.'

Walking across the floor, her heart was pounding. She couldn't wait to tell Josef what she'd heard. It wasn't much to work on but it was a start!

When Josef noted her arrival, he excused himself for a few moments.

'What is it?' he whispered.

The mechanics didn't appear interested in their conversation but Andrea didn't want to take chances. Surprisingly, in her excited state, her German vocabulary flowed as she repeated the mechanics' discussion.

'What do you think? she breathed, her pulse racing as he slid his arm around her shoulders and drew her aside.

'I can stretch this out until two o'clock. See if you can find out any more but please be careful, Andrea.'

'I'll go and find Vic. He's always pleased to see me.'

'Remember what I said. I don't want to see you hurt.'

'You're worrying about nothing!' she chortled, pulling away from him.

Maybe he wasn't, she thought, walking towards Vic's office area. There was a lot of money involved in this racing firm, millions in fact. Suddenly changing direction, she went to find her father's secretary for a short chat. It might look too suspicious if she went straight back to the mechanics to complete her low-key investigation.

When the subject of her father was raised during the course of their conversation, his secretary couldn't shed any light on his state of mind, and Andrea didn't want to press her too hard.

'I assumed his break in Austria would do him good,' the woman said, shrugging her shoulders. 'He was back in here for an hour and it was as though he'd never left.'

Using Josef's impatience as an excuse, Andrea went to the factory floor. One thing was certain — her father's problems had something to do with this firm.

'Hello, Vic,' Andrea said, pecking him on the cheek. 'I bet you didn't expect to see me again so soon.'

'And we'll be seeing a lot more of you now you're working for our new Number One driver,' he replied pulling out a chair for her by his desk.

'I'll be with Dad a lot so I can keep an eye on him. He's looking so tired, Vic.'

'All firms have their ups and downs. This company is his brainchild so when there's a hitch, he worries more than most.' Vic smiled over her shoulder.

Turning, she saw Uncle Tony was standing there.

'I heard my favourite niece was here.' He went over to give her a hug.

'Congratulations! How does it feel to

be a grandfather?'

'Old!' He chuckled heartily. 'Very old! Why don't I give Sharon a call? It wouldn't take you long to drive over to her house.'

'It'll have to wait. Josef and I fly back this afternoon. I'll let Dad know when we'll be staying over longer then perhaps we can organise a family evening.'

'Andy was just saying she's a bit concerned about Roy's health,' Vic said.

Her uncle looked into her eyes.

'I'd be the first to tell you if anything was wrong. He's not as young as he was and this is a stressful job. There are days when it gets to me, too.'

'Look, I must go.' Andrea glanced at her watch. 'But please call me if he starts to look worse.'

'Go back to Austria and enjoy your life there. Vic and I will watch over him.'

Feeling more optimistic about having the two men's backing, Andrea left the office but stopped on wondering whether Uncle Tony had her phone number. As she turned back, she noticed that they were having an animated discussion although their voices were hushed. Their parting smiles had disappeared and they appeared agitated by something. What on earth was going on?

They had un uneventful flight back to Austria, and the following night, once they'd got back from Erich's wedding, Andrea accepted Josef's offer of a nightcap and waited on the sofa while he fixed their brandies.

'You're still bothered about Roy?' he asked, handing her a glass.

'It's been getting to me since yesterday. I'm sorry if I was quiet today. It might have been better if you'd gone without me.'

'And let you stay here alone?' Josef sat beside her. 'Quiet or not, I was glad to have your company.'

'It doesn't make sense, Josef. Uncle Tony says I'm not to worry but hasn't he realised my dad's not well? He didn't seem to be taking it very seriously.'

'Do you trust him?'

'Of course I do!' Andrea was shocked. 'He's my uncle. There have been times when I've wondered whether he's jealous of my dad. He tries to go one better, with larger car, bigger house and holidays to exclusive resorts.' She shrugged. 'I can't say I've been close to my uncle. You never really know what he's thinking. Aunt Celie is like Dad. You can trust them and you can see what mood they're in by just looking at them. Neither of them is devious.'

'You think your uncle might be?'

'I shouldn't even be thinking that of a relation, Josef. Tony put his money into the company along with Dad. Why would he want the business to suffer?'

'We're only supposing that your uncle is involved. However we do know there have been problems with the receipt of spare parts.'

'I wish we could have stayed on

longer.' Andrea sighed deeply.

'Then let's give them a surprise visit. Nobody will be expecting us if we turn up first thing on Monday morning.'

'We can't keep flying to and fro. It'll cost a fortune!'

'Leave me to take care of the details. Your father needs our help and a few trips by jet to England are nothing in comparison to what he's given me over the years. His faith in me is immeasurable in monetary terms.'

'Thank you.' Leaning across, she pecked him on the cheek.

'Does this mean we're friends again?' he murmured when she reclined against the sofa cushions.

'I don't like fighting with you, yet I can't give you the kind of relationship you're after. I wish we could reach a compromise, Josef.'

'We can. We'll take each day as it comes, enjoying our friendship.' He grinned. 'Am I taking things too far if I ask for a hug?'

Setting down her glass on the coffee

table, she went willingly into his open arms and savoured this embrace. Tears pricked her eyelids. Her love was strong but she couldn't accept being one of his girlfriends. It had to be special for him, too. Until he gave up the others, there could only be a platonic friendship.

★ ★ ★

'You're not thinking of pulling out of your contract, are you?' her father gasped when they walked into his office just after ten o'clock.

'No.' Josef grinned. 'I've got a few things to sort out in London that I couldn't finalise on Friday. I've popped in here as I've got a couple of questions about our sponsors for the coming season.'

'I'll make myself scarce and leave you men to your business.' Andrea turned to Josef. 'Regardless of your schedule, I'd like some time with my dad before we leave.'

'Of course.' His back was towards her

father and she saw him mouth the words, 'Good luck.'

Strolling around the factory floor, Andrea listened out for any snippets of conversation above the piped music but there was nothing of interest. Steve seemed a bit uncomfortable with her arrival in his area so she moved on.

'Twice in one week?' Vic grunted when she bumped into him in the corridor. 'Josef must be taking his new position extremely seriously.'

'He could never be faulted on his dedication, Vic. You should remember what he was like.'

'We can do without him coming around every five minutes. The man will be working as hard for him as they do for any of our drivers.' With a snort of disgust, he scurried away, leaving Andrea startled by his unusually icy outburst.

Returning to her dad's office, Andrea was quiet while they drank mid-morning coffee.

'You're looking thoughtful, darling.'

'I'm trying to remember what other meetings we've got today.'

'Will you be able to stay for dinner? Your mum would love it if you could.'

Before either she or Josef could reply, there was a knock at the door. Vic and Tony entered, looking surprised to see them still there.

'We should be going, Andrea.' Josef got up and taking her arm, helped her to her feet. 'Sadly, we won't be able to accept your invitation, Roy. We're flying back to Austria today.' As she shook hands with the men, he added, 'Next time we visit, we'll call in advance so we can make a firm date.'

Once they were in his hired car, Andrea turned to face him.

'You told me to pack enough clothes for several days. What's going on?'

'Did you learn anything new?' Josef asked, ignoring her own question.

'No. Vic was a bit abrupt and the mechanics weren't very happy to see me.'

'I'm certain there's a cover-up going

on and that your father isn't involved in it.' Driving down the country lane, he pulled the car over beside a telephone box. 'I'll book us into a hotel in London for the night. We can't stay near here in case we're recognised.'

As he got out, she leaped from her seat and caught him up.

'I've got a better idea, Josef.' She held on to his arm.

Getting coins from her purse, she dialled the number of her old house. It turned out their luck was in. Dave was there as he'd worked shifts over the week-end and he said he'd be delighted to put them up for the night.

Arriving in the village, Josef said he really did have business in London and he left Andrea with Dave for the rest of the day. Shortly after six o'clock, he returned for the wonderful meal which Dave had prepared.

'It's a good thing that Mick and I haven't been able to agree on a housemate,' Dave said while they ate. 'You can have your old room, Andy.

There's a spare bed in Mick's room, Josef — if you want it.'

'Your sofa in the other room will be fine, thanks,' Josef replied.

'Am I allowed to ask you what's going on, Andy, or is it top secret?' Dave asked when she began to clear away their empty plates.

She looked at Josef and he nodded. While she dished out the portions of ice cream, she told Dave what they knew.

'If you two need to stay on, it won't be a problem and if there's anything Mick or I can do, just ask.' Dave glanced across at Josef. 'Andy's done a lot for us. You're a lucky man to have her with you.'

'I know that,' Josef responded with a smile.

Any uneasiness there had been up to that moment melted away and the men chatted as though they were old friends. Mick appeared later that evening and joined in the conversation about Josef's racing career.

'We should let you two get to bed,'

Dave suggested to Josef and Andrea at around ten-thirty. 'You've got a busy day tomorrow.'

Getting sheets, blankets and pillows from an upstairs cupboard, Andrea brought them down to Josef who was in the lounge.

'Will you be comfortable enough? I don't mind sleeping there — I'm not quite as tall as you are,' she said, shaking out the first sheet.

'You didn't say you had your own room here, Andrea.'

She slid the sheet over the sofa and tucked it in.

'You didn't ask me what the sleeping arrangements were. You were guilty of jumping to the wrong conclusion.' She faced him. 'There's never been anything other than friendship with either of my housemates. I let you believe Dave and I were a couple because I was hurt by your affair.'

'What affair, Andrea? There never was one.'

'I saw the pictures in the magazine

after I'd spoken to . . . ' She grabbed the top sheet and folded it in half. 'It doesn't matter. It's all over now, Josef.'

Quickly she made up the temporary bed and bid her good-night to him.

Once she was in bed, she lay looking up at the darkened ceiling. Why was love so painful? Picturing a mental image of Josef and Francine on New Year's Eve, she wondered why he was continuing to lie to her. If only he'd tell her what happened, she might begin to forgive him, though, like the proverbial leopard, would Josef never change his spots? Would he ever be content with the love of one woman?

9

'You had better answer that,' Josef said when Andrea entered the kitchen the following morning to find the phone ringing and Josef preparing a full breakfast for them both.

'Hello?' Andrea answered the call cagily. Listening for a few seconds, she held out the phone in Josef's direction. 'It's for you. It's your financial adviser in Innsbruck.'

'Thank you,' he said, taking the receiver from her grasp. 'The coffee is ready and your plate is keeping warm in the oven.'

While he spoke in German, which she didn't even bother to try to translate, Andrea poured herself some black coffee in an attempt to wake herself up.

'What's happening?' she asked when he joined her at the table and continued to eat his food.

'I tried to contact him yesterday but he was out for the day so I gave his secretary this number. I've asked him to check how quickly I can liquidise some of my investments.'

'Why?' Andrea's stomach was rumbling and she got up to fetch her plate.

Waiting until she sat down he replied, 'I want to know how much cash I can play around with. I realise you don't know much about your father's company, but do you know the percentage that is owned by Roy and your Uncle Tony?'

'I'm not sure if it's changed, Josef. They had twenty-six per cent each which made them the largest joint shareholder. This way they were able to have the final say in any company matter. What are you planning?'

'I've got to wait before I start building up your hopes, Andrea. But I should know by later today if this is feasible.'

'Please tell me!'

He grinned over at her.

'Patience, Liebling. You will find out in a short time.'

At two-thirty, Josef got his return phone call and afterwards he ordered Andrea to get her coat.

During the drive which she realised was to her father's premises, Josef refused point-blank to discuss his plans though she knew from the way he was humming along to the car radio he was pleased with himself. Relaxing in her seat, she felt more optimistic than she had in weeks.

'I thought you two had gone back to Austria!' Her dad was aghast as he got up from his chair and came to greet them. 'Don't get me wrong, I'm always happy to see you both. Can I get you coffee?'

'No, thank you,' Josef replied. 'I have a proposition to put to you, Roy. I know you usually don't like Andrea being around when confidential matters are being discussed but this time I'd like her to stay to hear my offer.'

'Then you'd both better sit down,'

her father said, showing them to the comfortable chairs reserved for visitors.

'For the past few months, Roy, I've been thinking about my life when I retire from racing. I've been looking around and I've decided that I'd still like to be involved in the sport.' He paused and the air was electrified, heavy with anticipation. 'Roy, there's no other team like yours and I'd like to buy into your company as an investment for my future.'

'Jo, I don't know what to say!' Her father's happiness was evident from his now beaming smile.

'I realise that it would have to be agreed by the rest of the board.'

'It would be a coup for the Thompson team given your status as a driver.' Her father's eyes were twinkling. 'I'll phone through for coffee.'

'We can't stay, Roy. You have my word that I'm serious in my intention although I won't sign any money over until an audit has been done of the books. The sum I intend to put up is large, so I hope it isn't a problem.'

'No,' her father replied. 'That's the way we usually do things.'

'Then we'll leave you to contact everyone concerned and we'll be in touch.'

'If you're going to be staying in England for a day or two, darling,' Roy said, pecking Andrea's cheek, 'perhaps you could come for dinner?'

'We'd like to — '

'But it's probably better if we don't mix socially until the negotiations are completed,' Josef cut in.

'OK. I'll start ringing them now.' Roy nodded sadly.

* * *

'I still can't understand why my dad looked so glum when we left,' she said to Josef while Dave was at the bar of their local pub getting the first round of drinks in.

After a lovely meal, the three of them had decided to go out so Josef could try the local brew. They were sitting at a corner table and Andrea smiled, noticing the strange looks they were getting from other customers. It was as if they couldn't quite place his well-known face.

'I hope I haven't stirred up more trouble for Roy,' Josef replied as Dave set a pint glass on the table in front of him. 'This was the only thing I could think of for getting nearer the truth.'

'Are you going to invest with him?' Andrea persisted, taking her drink.

'If the company books are sound, I will. Roy is one of the best mechanics in the business and given the right amount of capital, I'm certain the team's status would rise as would their drivers' positions on the starting grid next season.' He raised his glass. 'Cheers!'

'How about a game of pool?' Dave suggested. 'The table's empty.'

'I'll come and watch,' Andrea said, laughing. 'I know Josef always takes any game seriously and I don't want to get into a heated argument in here!'

Leaning against the wall sipping her drink, Andrea happily watched as the men played game after game. Their skills were evenly matched and neither wanted to concede defeat.

'I'm going back to the table. This is all getting too tense for me,' she said, unsure whether they'd heard her as they were engrossed in the competition.

Setting down at the table, Andrea gazed over at Josef as he shared a joke with her old friend. Momentarily he glanced over and winked at her. Her heart fell as she realised how empty her life would be without him to light her every waking second.

He knew the truth that there was nothing physical between herself and Dave, yet he hadn't brought the subject up today as she'd been hoping he would. Her dad's problems had to take priority though it wouldn't have hurt Josef to mention it in passing.

Walking back to the house with her arms threaded through those of the two of the dearest men in her life, she savoured Josef's touch more.

He declined Dave's offer of a nightcap.

'I'll see you in the morning.' Josef pecked Andrea's cheek as though she were a relative stranger. 'Sleep well.'

★ ★ ★

'What are we going to do?' she asked Josef, joining him for breakfast.

'We'll wait for an hour and see what's happened overnight.'

'What if everything's OK and the audit can go ahead?' Andrea sipped her strong coffee and noticed Josef shrug.

'Then we'll have to ask Roy directly what's worrying him.'

'I doubt he'd tell us.' Andrea raised her eyebrows.

The next hour was agonising and as the minutes ticked by, Andrea felt awash with coffee. Josef inhaled deeply.

'Call your father.'

'What shall I say to him?' she

asked, covering the mouthpiece as the switchboard operator was putting her through.

In a split-second Josef was beside her. Putting his arm around her shoulder, he bent his head so he could listen in. Her father's secretary answered the call.

'This is Andrea. Can you put me through to Dad, please?'

'I'm sorry, your father is very busy. I can get him to ring you back if you give me your number.' The woman's voice sounded edgy and a cold chill travelled down Andrea's spine.

Without waiting for a prompt from Josef, she countered, 'Tell him we're on our way now.' She hung up with trembling hands.

'Let's go,' he said, grabbing his car keys from the kitchen table and striding to the front door.

'I'm quite scared about all this, Josef,' Andrea murmured, doing up her seat belt the second he pulled away from the kerb.

'Whatever happens, I won't let

anything hurt you or your father. You have my word on that.'

'I want to see my father,' Andrea demanded, reaching his secretary's office.

'I gave him your message but he's still tied up.' The woman gave a sigh and indicated for them to take a seat. 'I can't say how long he's going to be.'

'What is going on?' Andrea persisted. 'Usually he'll talk to me, even if it's just for a minute.'

The secretary went over to the door and closed it so that they couldn't be overheard by anyone walking along the corridor. She turned around and leaned against the frame.

'Vic hasn't turned up for work today and your Uncle Tony is unavailable.'

'What do you mean unavailable?' Josef enquired.

'We've tried calling him at home and his answering machine isn't even switched on. His mobile has been turned off, too. He was supposed to have an appointment at nine-thirty and when I checked with the company for your father, they said he hadn't arrived nor had he phoned to cancel.' She gestured her bewilderment with upturned hands. 'He's just disappeared, Andy.'

'Can't I see Dad?'

'He's down on the factory floor at the moment. Last night he called in the accountants to audit the books and there's an urgent stocktake in progress.'

Andrea glanced at Josef.

'We were on the right track.' She returned her attention to the woman. 'Shall I drive over to my uncle's house? Maybe one of their neighbours might know something.'

'The matter's being dealt with by an expert, Andy.' The woman went over and poured coffee into two cups. 'You both look as though you could do with this,' she added, coming back and handing them over.

'Thank you,' Andrea said, exchanging a knowing look with Josef who had also drunk about a gallon of the stuff that morning!

Just when they'd managed to finish, her father appeared in the office.

'Have you been waiting long?' he asked, leading them into his office.

'We guessed something was wrong, Dad, so we decided to see for ourselves,' Andrea explained. 'Has there been trouble over the audit?'

'Sit down.' He sighed, going behind his desk and stretching his arms above his head when he was seated. 'I've been worried for some time, darling. When I spoke to your uncle, though, he assured me everything was OK. As he's always been better at figures than me, I believed him.' He shook his head. 'I should have got a second opinion but seeing as Tony's family, I didn't take it further.'

'What did the auditors find?' Josef asked.

'Almost immediately they found out there were discrepancies with the invoices for parts. I've spoken to Steve and he said fewer parts have been received these last few months than he remembered ordering.

'Someone has been cooking the books and it isn't hard to guess who's been behind this. We've had one of our major suppliers Fax us copies of the last invoices we supposedly sent to them and they don't tally with what we've got on record here. Somehow the money from the parts which should have been ordered — but which were never delivered as a substitute invoice for a lesser number had been sent to the supplier — has been moved from company funds.'

'Was it a large amount?' Josef enquired, leaning forward in his seat.

'A bit here and a bit there on every transaction has added up to a very tidy sum,' Andrea's father replied.

Just then, his secretary popped her head around the door.

'Your wife's on the phone. She's been around to Celie and Tony's house and nobody's answering the door. The neighbours say they think they heard a car revving up early this morning but there's been no sign of them today.'

'OK. Tell her I'll be home soon to speak to her.' Leaning his elbows on his desk, he held his head in his hands. 'I feel awful informing on my sister's husband, but I have to call the police.'

'You're sure Uncle Tony is to blame?'

'His disappearing act so soon after I mentioned having the books checked is a giveaway, as is Vic's absence today.' He tutted loudly. 'I shouldn't have devoted all my time to the technical side.'

Getting up, she went around his desk and slid her arm across his shoulders.

'Uncle Tony was the financial director. It was his line of expertise.'

'Wasn't it just! Through his and Vic's greed, they've destroyed this team. We'll be the laughing stock of the paddock, if we ever manage to get there. It won't be long before the rumours are confirmed and all our sponsors will begin pulling out. This is the end, Andy.'

She hugged him tightly and was startled when Josef said, 'Not necessarily, Roy!' Andrea listened to Josef with interest. 'I'm willing to put up the cash to cover the money that's gone missing but in return I'll expect to be given your brother-in-law's company shares. I would also want to be involved in all further decisions regardless of how trivial you think they may be.'

'You're going to have enough to concentrate on, Jo, at the start of the season in a new car.'

'If the real story is leaked to the Press, I mightn't have a ride this season at all. Neither of us wants to see the team go under. We want to raise the prestige of Thompson Racing. I may be taking over Tony's shares but I'll ensure the money goes into the company's bank account and not his.'

Andrea noticed that although her father had been through a traumatic experience, finding out he'd been swindled by someone he trusted, the colour was returning to his cheeks.

'Tony won't be happy if he finds out what's happened to his shares.'

'Dad! He's a cheat. He doesn't deserve your loyalty.'

'I agree with Andrea, Roy. Try to contact him if you can and explain what I've suggested. An innocent man will fight for what's his but somehow I don't think Tony will — that's if you can find him.' Josef got up from his chair. 'I'm going to have to return to Austria and speak to my financial adviser. I'll give Tony a week to make up his mind and by then I should have the contracts ready to be exchanged. Do you agree to my demands in principle, Roy?'

Her father rose and held out his hand. As they both shook on it, he replied, 'You lay out your terms and I'll ensure you're given the backing of the board.'

'One final thing,' Josef added as Andrea hugged her father goodbye. 'Can you arrange a high-profile Press conference for next Friday? Don't spare the cost. We want to show them we mean business this year.'

Walking to the car, Andrea aired her worries to Josef.

'Don't you think you're rushing this?'

'No.' He stopped and opened the doors with a flick of his key fob. 'We have to move quickly to diffuse the publicity as best as we can because the police will have to be notified. No doubt they're already on a beach in a country which doesn't have an extradition agreement with Britain. With Vic's assistance, Tony wasn't only robbing your father of money — he was stealing Roy's health as well.' His eyes narrowed. 'To me, that is unforgivable, Liebling.'

★ ★ ★

Once they arrived back in Austria, Andrea found they had a lot of work to catch up on. For the next two days, she had no difficulty keeping Josef's interest on business. As soon as he'd showered after his training session each morning, he would come into the office to either begin dictation or give her instructions on the morning's correspondence.

On Thursday and Friday they had dinner together then spent the rest of the evening chatting and listening to CDs in the lounge. It was almost like the old days except that Josef would relax in his armchair rather than sit beside her on the sofa. She was enjoying his company so much, she wished she hadn't turned him away at New Year. Now her father's troubles were practically sorted out, she knew it would only be a matter of time before hers and Josef's relationship was back on course. The chemistry between them was becoming stronger by the day. Comforted by these thoughts she slept very well on Friday night.

While Andrea was swimming the next morning, she was stunned to find Josef had turned up and was watching her from the side.

'When you've finished, Andrea, could you come into the office, please?' As she took a stroke towards the steps, he added, 'There's no rush. This can wait.'

She swam for another five minutes and then she couldn't bear it any longer. What did he want? Showering in the small changing room, she dressed quickly and towel-dried her hair then hurried along to see him.

'Is it another letter to do with Thompson Racing?' she asked, sliding into the chair opposite his desk.

'No, Andrea.' He lifted the top document from his tray and held it out to her. 'This is for you.'

Taking it, she frowned on scanning the first page.

'It's my employment contract.' Her sapphire eyes were saucer-wide as she met his gaze. 'Josef, what's going on?'

'Your services are no longer required, Liebling. Your contract has been terminated.'

10

But why?' Andrea gasped. 'Is there something wrong with my work? Why didn't you say something?'

He leaned back in his chair and crossed one leg over the other.

'You've exceeded my expectations and I wish every employee was as dedicated as yourself.'

'Then why are you firing me?' The signed contract trembled in her hands.

'Did I say that?'

'Why else would you be giving this back to me? You need a full-time secretary to take care of your business,' she insisted with fervour which was coming directly from her heart.

She couldn't bear another separation from him!

'We have achieved what we set out to do, Andrea. We've found out what your father's problems were and have rectified them.'

He flicked a tiny speck of dust from the leg of his jeans.

'Although you've tried to settle here, I've seen how unhappy you've been.'

She was in shock as he continued, 'I'll have your belongings shipped back to England on my private jet next week. Also I will see to it that you're paid in full for the trial period of six months.'

'There's no need, Josef,' she murmured, her lips quavering.

'It was written into the contract that if I terminated it within the first half-year then you would receive the salary for that period.'

His clipped accent became more mellow as he went on.

'Don't turn this down, Andrea. You need to have something to live on while you search for a job that you will really enjoy.'

Josef turned his attention to another folder and he seemed to forget she was in the room.

'When do you want me to leave?' she asked unsteadily, wishing that at any moment he'd give one of his beaming smiles and say that it was a practical joke.

Instead he shrugged nonchalantly.

'I can have the jet readied for later this afternoon if that will suit you.'

His words were like a blow to her stomach and she was glad she wasn't standing up otherwise she didn't think her legs would have supported her.

'Today?'

'You're welcome to stay the week-end if you want to pack your belongings yourself, although Frau Unger could be trusted if you're prepared to wait until she returns on Monday.'

His voice had become icy again and suddenly she felt she knew the real reason behind her hasty departure. His interest in her had waned. He had had fun with her while she was bound to him on the pretext of helping her father. Now the game was over. He wanted to get on to his next conquest and he'd feel uneasy with his ex-fiancée living in the same house.

'Why don't you call Dave and tell him you'd like your old room back?'

She got up, swallowing away the tight knot that had formed in her throat.

'I'll call him from the lounge so I don't disturb you.'

Getting to his feet, he towered over her.

'You won't be. I'm going to the gym for an extra session. I'll have to be ultra-fit this season otherwise I may have to replace myself with a better driver!'

His laughter didn't reach his eyes.

When he'd gone, she chewed on her bottom lip to stop herself sobbing. Taking a deep breath, she punched in the international dialling code then added the number of her old house.

'Dave? It's me, Andy,' she said, wiping away a tear from her cheek. 'I've got a favour to ask. Is my room still free?'

'Of course. Are you coming over to visit us again?'

Andrea waited for a few moments until her voice was calmer.

'No, I'm coming back to England for good.'

'What!' Dave cried down the phone. 'I thought you two were sorting out your differences.'

'So did I. But Josef's not as interested as I thought he was. He's terminated my contract and I can leave today.'

'Listen, why don't you tell me about it if you want to get it off your chest?'

Andrea sighed and repeated the conversation word for word, adding at the end, 'This has knocked me sideways, Dave.'

'Yes, I'm stunned myself. I didn't think he would let you go a second time.'

Perching on the desk, she smiled sadly down the phone.

'You're just an incurable romantic, Dave.'

'From some things he said when we

were playing pool and you'd gone back to our table, I believed you had a future together.'

'What did he say?' She sat bolt upright.

'I don't know if it'll help but here goes. The first thing was that Josef told me that he was hurt when you sent back his engagement ring.'

'He deserved it for what he did to me!'

'Listen, Andy. He also said that you're the only woman he's ever cared for. Don't you see? He's still in love with you.'

'Did he say that, too?' Andrea gasped.

'He didn't need to. I could see it in his eyes. The way he looked at you and spoke about you, Andy — it was pretty obvious he's smitten.' He paused for a few seconds. 'Do you love him?'

'I don't think I ever stopped loving him, Dave.'

'Then go and tell him now before it's too late!'

'But what if he laughs at me?' She gave another sigh.

'Andy, what have you got to lose? I don't think he will laugh at you, but even if he does, you can leave there today. Don't regret your silence for the rest of your life.'

'Maybe you're right, Dave,' Andrea said thoughtfully.

'You know I am.' Dave chuckled. 'Go and do it right now and call me back when you've talked to him. I'm sure you'll have good news.'

'And if I don't?'

'Then I'll meet you at the airport and you can give me a big kick on the shins for interfering!'

Once she'd put down the phone, she considered how best to approach the situation. Apologise? Blurt it out? How?

Feeling as courageous as she'd ever be, she strode down to Josef's gym and entered without knocking.

He was working on the weights machine and he stopped when he saw her.

'What do you want?'

'I didn't want to disturb you but this is important.'

Andrea swallowed as he got up and reached for his towel. Coming towards her, he wiped his glowing face.

'Have you sorted out everything with Dave?'

'More or less,' she replied, her nervousness coming back. It was now or never! 'Josef, I don't want to go to England. I've enjoyed working for you and I want to stay on here permanently.'

His gaze was unfathomable as it held hers. Humiliation caused tears to form in her eyes while this prolonged silence continued. Dave had been wrong in his assumption and she'd been stupid to believe him.

'Forget it,' she snapped. 'You don't want me here. I'll start packing now.'

Turning on her heels, she scurried towards the door though she was halted by his grasp on her arm when he caught her up.

'Why did you say that I want you to go?' he asked, pulling her around so she faced him.'

'It's obvious you don't want me to cramp your style with your married friend, Francine.'

'There's been nothing between me and that woman.'

'It didn't look like that on New Year's Eve!' she bit out.

His pressure on her arms increased.

'I'm letting you go from the contract because I saw how happy Dave has made you. You're ideally suited. I was wrong to come between you, Andrea. I hoped that by bringing you here, you would change your opinion of me. When you sent my ring back, I thought I'd still see you in the pit lane at the races. I didn't consider that you'd cut yourself off from the scene. I tried to forget you, Andrea, but I haven't succeeded.'

'Wasn't our engagement one of the serious errors of judgement that you talked about?'

'Are you kidding?'

Releasing his grip, he reached out and stroked her cheek.

'The two errors I made were letting you go in the first place.'

'And the second one?' she prompted breathlessly.

'Not coming after you sooner, Liebling.'

Andrea didn't fight him as he pulled her into his embrace and kissed her passionately. She responded, savouring his taste and touch though suddenly she drew back. Her eyes had widened in alarm on recalling his female visitor, Francine, all these years ago.

'What's wrong?' he enquired.

'It comes back to trust, Josef. If you love someone there has to be trust, too.'

His lips covered hers briefly.

'I've never stopped loving you, Andrea.'

She stepped back and glared at him.

'Then why did you make love to another woman while we were engaged?' she demanded.

'This is news to me! I was devoted to you.'

'While you were waiting for me to phone that night after my friend's wedding reception, you were with Francine. You don't have to deny it, Josef.'

'I swear to you, I have never gone near the woman!'

'Oh, really?'

Andrea repeated what she had learned on the telephone and of getting the engaged tone for the rest of the night.

Josef strolled to the table and picked up the bottle of mineral water. Taking a long drink, he returned to her with it clutched in his hand.

'I'd planned to have an early night but my friend Dieter arrived unexpectedly with his fiancée, Francine. I'd told him I was having the Ferrari delivered and he came over to see it. We were out of the house for fifteen minutes at the most. He's always been a Ferrari fan.'

Josef took another gulp of water.

'When you didn't call me, I guessed you had stayed on at the reception so after they went home, I went to bed as it was past midnight by then. The next morning I tried to phone you and the line was dead. I checked and found that the extension in my study was off the hook. I thought I'd knocked it accidentally when I'd gone in there the previous evening to find the photos of our holiday in Italy. Dieter wanted to know what you were like as he hadn't met you.'

Taking Andrea by the hand, he led her over to the bench and they sat down.

'I was awake most of that Saturday night trying to make one of the hardest decisions in my life.' Josef sighed. 'I'd been offered the contract to drive for the Italian company who were willing to pay me a fantastic salary. Your father, too, wanted me to extend my contract at Thompson Racing for another season, although the money was less than the Italians were offering. I had to decide what was more important — money or loyalty to the man who believed in me.'

'And you took the money.'

'I didn't intend to, Andrea, but I thought harder after you had flown into a rage the next day which seemed to be over nothing.'

Taking her hand in his he squeezed it.

'You're the only woman I've loved, even if at times you are like a spitfire!'

'I had just cause that day, Josef. Francine said some terrible things to me and they hit a nerve. Maybe I'd have questioned things further if I hadn't seen that photo of you with that woman. You hadn't pressed me on going to the Far East and Australia with you and I assumed it was because you wanted your freedom. I sent the ring back before you could hurt me any more.'

'Come with me.'

Josef brought her to her feet and, sliding his arm around her waist, led her to his study which was located opposite their office.

'Won't you get cold like that?'

She pointed to his T-shirt which was damp from his strenuous training.

'This won't take long and I'll shower afterwards. I want you to know the truth so that it won't come between us again.'

Holding hands they were facing one another.

'Francine is a nasty woman. She was engaged to Dieter but she'd make insinuations on the quiet that she'd drop him if I was interested in her. She'd caught me alone in the kitchen that Saturday night and told me this. I told her I already had a fiancée whom I loved.'

'How did she know so much about me?'

'I told Dieter some bits and pieces that evening.'

'And the bit about you getting the drive because of me?'

He grasped her fingers tightly.

'I told him some people might have thought that was the reason for our relationship but I insisted it wasn't. I said we were together because we were in love. Francine twisted my words. She must have been annoyed by the rejection so decided to lash out at you.'

'She certainly did that!'

'She dumped Dieter a few weeks later for an older man who had plenty of money. She divorced him and is now on her second husband.'

'The man who was with her at New Year?' she enquired.

Josef nodded.

'I feel sorry for him and I don't even know him.'

'Why were you so pleasant to her when she'd been so nasty to your friend, Dieter?'

'If you remember, I knew most of the people in that hall that evening and it was easier to be polite to Francine for a few minutes than have an argument and give the village gossips plenty to talk about for the next year. My family still lives in the area so it might have made things awkward for them. I didn't want that to happen.'

Andrea raised her eyebrows.

'You were being extremely polite on the dance floor!'

'Andrea, she was drunk. She could barely stand up.'

'You men can be so gullible,' she responded with a smile.

'If you're going to insult me, Liebling, I won't show you what I was going to.'

He chuckled, letting go of her hands.

'What is it?' she asked, watching him go over to the wall.

He spun around.

'Take back the gullible and I won't call you nosy!'

'OK,' she said, nodding.

Josef pushed aside a painting to reveal a wall safe. Entering a combination, he opened the metal door and brought out a small box. Going over to her, she recognised the box which she hadn't seen for years and she held her breath.

'This is for you,' he said, opening the box to reveal the diamond and sapphire ring lying on the bed of satin. 'I've kept it hoping that you'd wear it again.'

In awe, she stared down as he took her hand and slipped the ring over her finger. The gems sparkled in the sunlight coming through the window.

'Andrea, I want us to make a fresh start. If this ring hold bad memories for you, then we'll choose another.'

'No, I love it — I always have,' she murmured, unable to take her gaze from her now trembling hand.

His fingers caught her chin and raised it to meet his kiss. She responded enthusiastically and was shocked when it was Josef who pulled back from her this time.

'There's one final thing you should know, Leibling.'

He stroked her hair as he spoke.

'Your father was aware of my real reason for moving to Italy and not staying with his team. I wanted to disprove allegations that I'd been using you to climb up the career ladder. He understood that I wanted to prove my own worth to everyone — but most importantly to you.'

'The salary had nothing to do with it?'

He looked her directly in the eye as he replied, 'No, I wanted you to know that our love was real. Is very real,' he added in a murmur against her lips when their passionate caresses continued.

'I should call Dave and tell him to let the room!'

'Later, Andrea. We have four years to make up for.'

★ ★ ★

The Press conference was being held on the factory floor of Thompson Racing's premises so that the large number of journalists could be accommodated. At one end there were tables laden with a magnificent buffet and plenty of drinks to keep the gathered media personnel happy. At the other end of the room, a low stage had been set up.

In between were rows of chairs and from her position beside her father and Josef at the table on the stage, Andrea noticed that most of them were occupied.

She smiled at her father as he got to his feet. He looked much more relaxed even though they hadn't yet found Uncle Tony or Vic. The police had been brought in and fortunately the matter was being dealt with discreetly.

There was a hush when her father began to speak.

'Thank you for all coming today.'

Andrea was blinded by the barrage of flashlights but she fought to keep her eyes open.

'This is an important day for Thompson Racing. At the end of last season, we announced that Josef Meyer would be returning to our team as our Number One driver.

'From the first of February, Josef will be a major shareholder of the company. Full details of his investment are given in the Press release which my staff are distributing to you now. I'm pleased to say that following the unforeseen retirement of my brother-in-law, we will be keeping this within the family.'

Josef covered her hand with his as her father beamed down at them.

'In my capacity as father of the bride-to-be, I'm delighted to announce that my daughter Andrea and my very good friend Josef are getting married next month!'

There was a round of loud applause and Andrea beckoned for her mum, who was standing at the side of the stage, to join them. When she did, there were more flashes.

'Josef, isn't this announcement rather sudden?' one of the Press men called out.

'Are you referring to my marriage or my investment?' he queried in jest.

'Both,' the man replied.

'My reasons for investing in Thompson Racing are detailed in the Press release. As to a hasty wedding, Andrea and I want as much time together as we can manage before the racing season begins. We have known one another for five years and we don't want to spend any more time apart.'

She clasped his hand as he and her father answered several other general questions.

'There's champagne being poured,' her father said, waving his hand to the back of the room. 'We'd like you to join us in celebrating both ventures.'

Her mother and father went to circulate with the media people so Andrea and Josef were finally alone.

'Do you think everything will be ready by next month?' she asked him with a worried expression on her face. 'It's a lot to organise in so short a time.'

Smiling, he bent forward and kissed her on the lips.

'With your mother arranging things here and mine currently working overtime on them in Austria, we've no worries, Liebling.'

'Two weddings is rather extravagant!'

'This way nobody will be missed out and your mother will be able to buy two hats — one for the English ceremony and another for our blessing in Austria.' He frowned. 'You're not having second thoughts, Fräulein Thompson?'

She put her arms around his neck.

'Never. I love you, Josef and I couldn't live without you. I'm so glad that you employed me and I was able to see what I was missing.'

'Are you sure you want to continue as my assistant?'

'I'm looking forward to travelling the world with you. In a few years, it mightn't be easy if we have children.'

He stroked her hair tenderly.

'And that's the only reason you're coming with me? You're not keeping an eye on me?'

'Somebody has to ensure your paperwork is kept up-to-date,' she chided lovingly. 'I trust you implicitly.'

'Are you sure?' He smiled.

'I have no doubts. I wouldn't have agreed to marry you, otherwise.'

She slid her arm through his.

'Shouldn't we join in the celebration?'

As they walked down the room, she couldn't wait for the moment when they'd be strolling together down the aisle. Like their mutual trust, she knew their love would never falter.

THE END

We do hope that you have enjoyed reading this large print book.

Did you know that all of our titles are available for purchase?

We publish a wide range of high quality large print books including:
Romances, Mysteries, Classics
General Fiction
Non Fiction and Westerns

Special interest titles available in large print are:
The Little Oxford Dictionary
Music Book, Song Book
Hymn Book, Service Book

Also available from us courtesy of Oxford University Press:
Young Readers' Dictionary
(large print edition)
Young Readers' Thesaurus
(large print edition)

For further information or a free brochure, please contact us at:
Ulverscroft Large Print Books Ltd.,
The Green, Bradgate Road, Anstey,
Leicester, LE7 7FU, England.
Tel: (00 44) **0116 236 4325**
Fax: (00 44) **0116 234 0205**

VISIONS OF THE HEART

Christine Briscomb

When property developer Connor Grant contracted Natalie Jensen to landscape the grounds of his large country house near Ashley in South Australia, she was ecstatic. But then she discovered he was acquiring — and ripping apart — great swathes of the town. Her own mother's house and the hall where the drama group met were two of his targets. Natalie was desperate to stop Connor's plans — but she also had to fight the powerful attraction flowing between them.

FINGALA, MAID OF RATHAY

Mary Cummins

On his deathbed, Sir James Montgomery of Rathay asks his daughter, Fingala, to swear that she will not honour her marriage contract until her brother Patrick, the new heir, returns from serving the King. Patrick must marry. Rathay must not be left without a mistress. But Patrick has fallen in love with the Lady Catherine Gordon whom the King, James IV, has given in marriage to the young man who claims to be Richard of York, one of the princes in the Tower.

ZABILLET OF THE SNOW

Catherine Darby

For Zabillet, a young peasant girl growing up in the tiny French village of Fromage in the mid-fourteenth century, a respectable marriage is the height of her parents' ambitions for her. But life is changing. Zabillet's love for a handsome shepherd is tested when she is invited to join the La Neige household, where her mistress, Lady Petronella, has plans for her grandson, Benet. And over all broods the horror of the Great Death that claims all whom it touches.

PERILOUS JOURNEY

Caroline Joyce

After the execution of Charles I,
Louisa's Royalist father considers it
too dangerous for her to stay in
England and arranges for her to go
to the Isle of Man with Armand de
la Tremouille, the nephew of the
island's Royalist Governor. Their
ship is boarded by Parliamentarians
who plan to sail for Ireland, but a
storm causes them to be ship-
wrecked on the Calf of Man.
Magnus Stapleton, the Parliamen-
tarian chief, becomes infatuated
with Louisa, but she has fallen in
love with Armand.